OUR VIRTUAL LOVE STORY

OUR VIRTUAL LOVE STORY

Juhi GP

Srishti
PUBLISHERS & DISTRIBUTORS

Srishti Publishers & Distributors
A unit of AJR Publishing LLP
212A, Peacock Lane
Shahpur Jat, New Delhi – 110 049
editorial@srishtipublishers.com

First published by
Srishti Publishers & Distributors in 2022

10 9 8 7 6 5 4 3 2 1

This is a work of fiction. The characters, places, organisations and events described in this book are either a work of the author's imagination or have been used fictitiously. Any resemblance to people, living or dead, places, events, communities or organisations is purely coincidental.

Printed and bound in India

Dedicated to
my friends and family in India,
who I miss dearly.

Acknowledgement

There are many people who supported me through the journey of my debut novel. I want you all to know that your contribution means a lot to me.

Starting with my beta readers, Shilpa, Akshara, Natasha, Kathan, Sanjana and Sonia, who gave me consistent feedback for every chapter.

My parents, sister and friends Nikhil and Disha for their endless support.

To my professional mentors Ryan, Natalie and Laura, who inspired me to achieve this cherished dream.

Special credits to Dipti Patel and Akash Menon for believing in my literary talents and the story of Samira and Rishabh.

To team Srishti – Arup, Vini and Stuti who worked closely with me to refine the story and share it with the world.

To countless other cheerleaders who motivated me to keep going and finish the story,

And lastly, to all those out there who are playing video games!

Prologue

'Hold fire! I've got supplies!' Rishabh screamed as he called out to his teammates in the platoon. He reached out and handed them some extra ammunition.

They were in the midst of a dense forest, somewhere in Eastern Europe, fighting a heated war.

'What more do you guys need?' Rishabh asked exasperated.

'A 5.66 mm, please,' heaved Salman.

'7.62 mm,' Gautam declared in the same moment.

'Here you go,' Rishabh threw the rifles their way.

'Thanks, Captain,' came the swift response from both.

Rishabh wiped his brow as he braced himself for the next move.

'Enemies at 150 coordinates, hiding behind rocks. I say let's push,' Akash's impatient voice boomed.

'Thunder! Can you look through the scope before we push?' asked Rishabh. He wanted to make sure his sniper was able to analyse the situation carefully before making any hasty decisions.

'Don't you trust me?' Akash sounded almost diffident.

'No, not at all,' Rishabh declared honestly. He was the strategic one in the group, and thus their "Captain".

Before the sniper could gauge the situation, Akash prematurely ventured out towards the enemy's location in a very filmi style. He was shot and knocked out by an enemy snaking in the grass, all within a matter of seconds.

'Help! Help!' he cried in desperation.

The remainder of the squad was forced to move forward hastily in order to save him. Rishabh tossed a smoke grenade to mask their movements, but like any unplanned strategy that ends up badly, they too were quickly spotted by the enemies and killed.

Better luck next time! Second place. The prompt was displayed on the screen.

'Hey, we almost had them there. Nice game, boys!' How's the *josh*?" exclaimed Akash, trying to salvage the situation.

'Not high sir,' came the response in unison.

1

Battle of Arstov (BOA)

'Jeez Akash!' complained Rishabh as he slid his fingers down his mobile phone screen. He was now done with navigating through his character's movements. Their engineering squad had been playing the intense mobile game of Battle Of Arstov (BOA) which was royally screwed over by none other than Mad Dog, a.k.a Akash.

The four friends – Rishabh, Gautam, Salman and Akash stuck to their trendy names whilst playing BOA wherein Rishabh was Kraken, Akash was Mad Dog, Gautam was Big Papa and Salman was Annihilator .

'Fuck! You got us killed, bro!' groaned Gautam.

'Why do you *always* do this, bro?' exclaimed Salman, expressing his disappointment. 'We could have won. We were so close this time,'

'Sorry *yaar*,' Akash sounded genuinely sad. 'I just wanted to go for the kill, you know!'

This was a regular occurrence with Akash, something the rest of them had accepted and yet, had a hard time accepting. He became so reckless sometimes.

'Patience is a virtue, my friend. Nevermind! Anyone up for one more game?' Rishabh asked enthusiastically.

'I gotta go,' Salman said dejectedly, signing off. 'Mom's calling for lunch,'

'Okay. Bye, bro,' Rishabh mumbled as he stretched out his arms, flexing his body to get a break from the prolonged sitting.

'One second boys, BRB,' he said to the rest of his gang.

They had been playing on Las deszczowy – a map based in Scandinavia and were running up a hill. The game was down to the last ten players and in truly royal battle fashion; the map had started shrinking at a speedy rate, forcing the remaining players to confront each other.

There could only be one winner in BOA. The rules were simple. The kingdom of Arstov consisted of a few islands – Las deszczowy (rainforest), Góra (mountainous terrain) and Metel (Ice). Each island was distanced from the other and had a different terrain – rainforest, mountains and ice. The islands were separated by water full of sea monsters and so the players could not escape without surviving each island.

The kingdom of Arstov was also governed by the serpentine family. And so, each island was designed as spirals, with the map continuing to constrict players, as a BOA constrictor would. Once a map was selected, a hundred avatars of players spawned and got into an airplane. They could jump off any place on the map on the plane's route. Once they landed using their parachutes, they had to scramble for weapons, health kits and other items in order to kill any player they encountered until there remained one player or squad that gained victory.

As the game continued, the playable area on the map constricted in spiraling formations at regular intervals in order to dissuade players from hiding or "camping" in gaming terms. If you chose to stay in the zone outside of the BOA's spirals, which was essentially outside of the play zone, then the game hampered your health, eventually killing your character. If you survived a map, you proceeded to the next map where you competed with players who survived the first in various rounds and so the competition got tougher. Eventually, if a player or team survived all three islands, they were awarded the "Moccasin Assassin" title.

For the BOA players, the true goal of the game is to survive as long as possible rather than get the most kills. However, kills to death ratio (K/D, which is the number of kills you get in all your games compared to the number of times you die) is considered a matter of pride for a majority of testosterone-filled players so it is of equal importance.

❖

It was a rainy Saturday afternoon in Mumbai and so, a large number of people opted to stay indoors. However, the roads were blocked, with cars stuck in traffic as city dwellers tried to navigate their way at an extremely slow pace. Mumbai is indeed a city that never sleeps!

Rishabh gazed out of the window from his apartment building in Mahim, which was a predominantly Maharashtrian neighborhood in suburban Mumbai. He heard the pitter-patter of raindrops gaining intensity. Aside from the growing thunder, the piercing shrieks of cars honking urged him to close the window.

Definitely not going out today, he thought.

With the growing popularity of BOA in India, spending hours playing the game indoors was a great alternative to stepping outdoors.

Rishabh was perfectly happy to continue playing all day with his friends who were living with him during his engineering days. He remembered the fun moments in college when the boys in the hostel placed weekly wagers in the form of BOA tournaments. The losers had to sponsor the booze for the upcoming weekend. The tournaments would get pretty heated but some killjoys had complained to the administration, which is why the game was banned on the campus. Unfortunately, for them, they were dealing with a bunch of engineers who were easily able to set up a masked private server that allowed them to continue playing.

It had been six months since graduation. Rishabh's group of friends had dispersed from Mumbai, depending on where their jobs took them. Rishabh and Akash got placements in Mumbai itself so they still met regularly, but BOA was a great way to stay in touch with the rest of the group.

Rishabh returned to his silver Samsung Galaxy and put his headset back on. The avatars were in the game lobby, with the game's theme song playing in the background. As his headphones touched his ears, familiar voices continued through in the game chat. Akash was bragging about how he was eating a dozen eggs daily and as a result, his biceps had already grown an inch. Rishabh grinned to himself as he imagined Akash flexing and staring at himself in the mirror as he spoke.

'OK, I'm back guys,' Rishabh interrupted the conversation.

'How long do you take bro?' complained Akash.

'Why didn't you use the time to do some push-ups? Then, maybe those chicken stick arms of yours would actually grow,' Rishabh declared sarcastically.

Gautam chuckled loudly.

'Bro,' Akash started saying something but Rishabh cut him off.

'Okay, what do you guys want to play? We're down a player so I'll set it on auto-matching. That way, a random fourth player can join the team. Cool?'

Gautam chimed in, 'Let's play! Góra on the North American server!'

'Done. Let's go boys!' said Rishabh, tapping the necessary controls. Góra was the toughest map in BOA but Rishabh and his friends had unlocked it months ago since amateurs had no access to it.

As the game loaded, the fourth player's name popped up. "xxBrownSwanxx", it read. This person had a female avatar so Rishabh wondered if it was a girl. Guys donning female avatars, especially wearing only bras, existed in abundance in the gaming world. So he didn't put much thought into it. However, Akash being extremely shameless, kept hitting the "Turn on voice chat" voice command to get Brown Swan to speak.

Akash continued to provoke Brown Swan by singing "Turn on voice chat" but they didn't give in.

Rishabh couldn't blame them because Akash was being very annoying. If it really was a girl, his friends were just acting like creepy boys, the kind which women typically dealt with online.

'Leave Swan alone and focus on the game,' Rishabh interjected with an irritated tone.

'Oh boy! Someone's trying to get protective already. Should I call her *bhabhi*?' teased Akash.

As the boys were engaged in pointless banter, the screen showed that Brown Swan had already killed three enemies.

'Woah, she turned out to be a player!' gasped Akash.

Since they were conversing in Hindi and playing the North American server, Rishabh assumed that Brown Swan was a non-Indian person who didn't understand them. So he let Akash be.

Rishabh navigated his avatar towards Brown Swan and dropped a first-aid kit so she could replenish her character's health after engaging in that battle.

'Sister-in-law?' Akash continued teasing as he also moved his avatar towards them.

He pressed an emote so his character was dancing in order to tease them further. Brown Swan promptly tossed a frag grenade in his direction, killing his character instantly. Gautam and Rishabh roared with laughter as Akash stayed dumbstruck with embarrassment. The only words he could conjure up were 'What the...,'

'Take that, *bro*,' a female voice resonated with a sarcastic emphasis on "bro".

'Happy now?' she continued, this time in Hindi.

Oh God! thought Rishabh. *She's Indian!*

She had understood every word! Her voice was slightly deep with a hint of an American accent which made it sound pretty sexy. She might've been someone who immigrated there but had spent some time in India because her accent sounded very hybrid.

The game continued and ended quickly with Akash pulling out of the game after his embarrassing encounter and Gautam leaving shortly after he was eliminated.

Rishabh didn't want the same fate as Akash's, so despite his curiosity, he only communicated with Brown Swan to coordinate the game. Once the game ended, he was sure that his friends would send a friend request to her, but he couldn't really make up his mind on it.

However, Rishabh was pleasantly surprised when he saw her name pop up on his friend request list. He immediately accepted her request and then later, found her online. He even tried his luck by sending her a game invitation. Who would have thought that she would accept it instantly!

2
Brown Swan

Rishabh stared at the game's lobby area on his phone screen in anticipation.

Brown Swan's avatar appeared promptly. She was wearing one of the limited edition game outfits – a red bra with a black leather, cropped vest and a metallic belt around the rib cage, revealing washboard abs. It was very reminiscent of Xena, the warrior princess. Her look was complete with a leather jacket draped around her waist, black shorts, knee-length, lace-up combat boots and fingerless gloves which were clutching a machine gun.

Woof! She looked sexy!

Rishabh's avatar on the other hand, paled in comparison. He just wore a black and white checkered shirt with camo pants and grey school shoes. These were some of the free items available in the game.

Okay, she either paid generously for this stuff or she's just a damn good player and unlocked it, he thought. Either way, he was impressed.

'Hey, sorry about your friend,' Brown Swan's voice had a husky tone.

'No need to be sorry. That was epic!' Rishabh replied as he moved over to his bed and lay down. He was sure that she could hear him smile through the phone.

'Okay then, I'm not sorry!' she giggled. 'He was being such a dick so I had to troll him,'

'Haha! Thanks!' said Rishabh. He pressed the wave emote so his avatar could wave out to her.

'Yeah, you seem cool. Probably the *only* one out of that lot!'

'LOL! Thanks! They're not so bad actually. I've known them forever. So, where are you from?' he asked inquisitively.

'Well, from India originally, but I have been living in the States for a while now,'

'Where in the States?'

'California,'

'Nice....so...' He was about to say something when she interrupted.

'Wait! Let me invite another friend,'

A third player joined their lobby in the game. This person had a male avatar with a Romanian flag and was wearing a red checkered shirt and camo pants. It looked almost identical to Rishabh's avatar.

Rishabh immediately rummaged through the limited inventory of his avatar's outfits to dress it differently. The other player did the same thing.

'Personal jinx guys!' Brown Swan sounded amused.

Damn! She's a smart one. Rishabh thought, feeling a little self-conscious.

The other player spoke up.

'How've you been Swan?'

He had a thick South American accent.

'*Muy Bien,* El Padron,' she replied to him, addressing him by his gamer name.

Wow, she speaks Spanish too! Rishabh wondered if they were friends in real life.

'Metel ok?'

'Sure,' they echoed, complying obediently.

As they waited to board the virtual plane in the game, Padron grabbed the opportunity to ask, 'So what's your name?'

'Call me Swan,' she said, brushing off his curiosity instantly.

Rishabh had wanted to ask the same question but was glad he wasn't subjected to this mild humiliation. He decided not to probe any further.

Well at least they're not friends in real life, he thought.

They played a couple more rounds until El Padron had to retire.

'Okay, it's my last game Kraken,' said Brown Swan, letting out an audible yawn.

'What time is it out there?'

'Almost 4 a.m.'

'What? No work tomorrow?' gasped Rishabh. He quickly realised he shouldn't have assumed.

'Yeah, I do. But I hate Mondays and I hate my job,' she said in a matter-of-fact manner. Her tone was melancholic.

'Let's make this a good one,' she said, quickly shifting the focus back to the game.

'Hell yeah!' he said, sitting up in bed.

He tried to protect her in the game but she didn't need it. She eliminated enemy after enemy with her virtual assault rifle as Rishabh watched in admiration. Unfortunately, they were killed off towards the end and came fifth in the game.

'Aww, so close!' she groaned. 'Good game! See you tomorrow,'

'Good night,' said Rishabh and left the game after Swan.

He spent a few seconds analysing his strange attraction to this virtual entity. He found it rather odd. She could be anyone.

What if it's a dude? What if she's some fifty year old woman? His eyes widened in tandem with the drop of his jaw. He didn't realize he was staring at a mirror while thinking all this. He laughed at his confused reflection and continued his day in real life, forgetting about the virtual encounter.

Akash rang post dinner.

'Come over for a smoke session, bro!' he said. 'Also, bring the prototype along with you, I want to see it!' he signed off.

3
Saloni's Story

Saloni unpacked the remaining items out of her suitcases as two maids scampered around, arranging her shoe closet.

She owned at least fifty pairs of shoes. Her closet was nothing short of extraordinary. The Louboutins were neatly tucked on the top shelf, revealing signature red bottoms clearly visible through the glass shelves of the closets that housed them. Her Louis Vuitton and Gucci handbags dangled from the sides. The lower levels of her closet shelves were filled with all kinds of footwears arranged neatly by category – pumps, flats, stilettos, boots, booties, shooties – you name it, she had it.

Saloni owned enough shoes to sport a new pair every day for a whole month-and-a-half. And, this was just her footwear collection we're talking about! Her wardrobe closet was straight out of the Hollywood classic *Clueless*.

It took three days for her staff to assemble her new room. But Saloni was accustomed to this. What excited her more was the opportunity to explore a new place. She had lived in Kolkata her whole life, within the soft cocoon of her conservative yet doting parents' care. She belonged to a traditional Marwari family. Her father, Ramesh Goenka, was a shipping magnate, and her mother, Aparna was a homemaker.

She had an older brother, Akash, who went to IIT Bombay to pursue mechanical engineering. Later, he started working as a consultant for Oxford Street Financial Services in Mumbai.

'My son is an IITian,' he gloated, with a classic Indian head shake to any Bengali person who had ears. Akash was her father's pride.

Mr Goenka seemed to generate some sort of an inexplicable complex whenever he found himself in the midst of Bengalis. No amount of money he made could douse the flames of his once-burnt ego anytime he attempted to strike an intellectual conversation with them. The seeds of this complex were sown on the day of a parent-teacher conference when Ramesh went to Akash's school and tried to partake in a conversation about the political happenings in the country. But, he stopped when he heard discreet laughs turn into loud roars. Mr Goenka had turned red in the face, disturbing his finely combed moustache. He dragged his wife out of the school, interrupting her kitty-party conversation with some of the other students' mothers at the conference. He vowed to reverse this humiliation by ensuring that Akash attended one of the IITs someday. Akash was quickly pulled out of his football team and enrolled in engineering classes. When Mr Goenka was called down for Akash's misdemeanours as a result of an elaborate prank that he pulled at his tuition, he arranged for private tuitions for him with an IIT graduate.

'Why enroll in a shared education system when you can get the very best minds of IIT to privately tutor?' Mr Goenka scoffed, in an attempt to downgrade the parents of the kids who went to group classes. No amount of philandering on Akash's part angered Mr Goenka. For ultimately, he just cared about his son getting into IIT. He didn't care how he got there.

'Consider it as a token of appreciation,' he said, attempting to bribe Atul Banerjee, Akash's private tutor, into taking Aakash's JEE exam.

'Sir, Akash will get in by himself,' Atul said uncomfortably.

Mr Goenka stroked his pot belly and raised his eyebrows.

'And if he doesn't?' Goenka challenged.

'I promise,' Atul stuttered.

'Okay! It better work because you see these papers here I have...,' he said, waving the ownership papers of Atul's parents' house in his hands.

'Yes sir, don't worry,' Atul promised in desperation, sweating profusely.

Saloni witnessed all of this and mostly rolled her eyes. She found her father's bullying acts very childish.

What use is an IIT degree if you end up getting bullied by undereducated and middle-aged businessmen? She found the whole situation ironic.

However, unlike her brother she had restrictions. She was enrolled in an all-girls school, St. Michael's for Girls, with limited freedoms. Despite being an academically bright student, her parents never paid heed to her intelligence. But she knew she had a place in her father's heart. He spoiled her beyond limits by buying her fancy clothes and shoes from lands faraway.

Saloni quickly learned that if you can't beat the system, you must join it. Instead of protesting their outright sexism, she egged her parents on by following their rules and accepting their gifts wholeheartedly. She used the power of money to pave her way to popularity in school. For instance, while the other students distributed simple candies like Cadbury's Eclairs, Mango Bites and even *mithai* to their friends on their birthdays, Saloni was known to hand out mini hampers of Ferrero Rocher, Jolly Ranchers and Hershey's Kisses on hers. On the birthday of a close friend, she'd convince her father to throw private sleepovers for her buddies, complete with catered dinners and private movie screenings. Over the years, she continued to outsmart her parents in all spheres except one.

Saloni was strictly kept away from boys. All her life, she was only enrolled in women's institutions. Her brother, on the other hand, was allowed everything. He mostly disappeared at night after a long day of tuitions. Once, he came home late at night and retired to his room. Saloni observed him sniffing his fingers as if smelling the aromas of finely cooked butter chicken.

'Bro, I fingered Pooja,' she heard him telling some friend on the phone.

Saloni wondered what was so special about her wannabe brother. He managed to pave his way into IIT. To celebrate his achievement, her father threw a massive party in Kolkata, complete with resplendent fireworks that coalesced with the sky. Yet, Akash, as usual, engaged in debauchery with some friends and ended up getting a girl pregnant. The matter was quickly swept under the rug by none other than Mr Goenka. There was no way *this* was getting in the way of his carefully massaged ego.

Saloni developed a huge crush on Akash's tutor Atul, a smart guy with wasted intelligence, or so she thought. She used her charms and beauty to flirt with Atul and successfully sneaked him into her room one evening while the family was out. When they were caught kissing, Atul's hand was inside Saloni's blouse. He was swiftly escorted out, but Mr Goenka refused to end his tutoring services, for Akash was making great progress. Instead, he just moved them to a different location. That night Saloni cried, feeling defeated for the first time. *Why could her brother get away with anything?*

But she made up her mind to conquer the situation. She wasn't particularly close to Akash but she decided he was going to be her ticket to freedom.

'But Akash bhaiya will be there,' she stated, seeking permission for a night out, looking up at Akash coyly.

'Yes dad. It's okay,' Akash would reply coolly, unaware of his sister's conniving mind.

That was the beginning of her new adventure.

Akash's path was set. IIT Bombay, followed by two years of consulting, IIM Ahmedabad for post-graduation and eventually taking over the Goenka family business. He didn't seem to mind it at all, given the large sums of money he was given as incentive in exchange for massaging his father's ego.

All roads in Saloni's life would lead to a traditional arranged marriage but she was determined to taste the forbidden fruit before that happened.

❖

When Akash graduated from IIT, her father rented a posh, sea-facing, three-bedroom apartment in Mumbai's elite Worli Sea Face neighborhood. The Ambanis and Piramals had invested in a mansion in close proximity. The apartment was furnished and staffed with two maids and a cook. Akash was free to bring home women and friends to smoke weed. (with or without his parents' knowledge).

As these events ensued, Saloni turned twenty-one. It was finally time to enact her plan. She secretly applied to Sophia College in Mumbai for a Master's programme. She tore up applications of colleges she pretended to apply to in Kolkata. Sophia was a women's college as well, but that part of her plan was only to appease her parents. Her true mission was to get out of Kolkata, out of her parent's reach.

When the letter of acceptance arrived, Saloni was quick to bring up the subject before they suspected anything.

'But Akash bhaiya is there,' she said, speaking of Mumbai. 'Can't I stay with him?' she asked innocently.

When Akash assured his parents of her safety and well-being, she was allowed to go to Mumbai and live with him on certain conditions. But Saloni was unnerved by this because fooling her brother was easy.

❖

The maids finally completed the room arrangements.

Saloni was satisfied. She put on a silk robe and fluffy room slippers and took a deep breath, tasting the sweet scent of freedom. She turned on her sound system and Ariana Grande's *Thank You, Next* started playing. She started dancing candidly with her eyes closed.

When she came to her senses, she caught a pair of eyes smiling at her in the doorway. It was a young man.

'Hi,' he said, letting out a giggle.

Embarrassed, she sprinted to slam the door.

4

Bawarchi

Saloni peered outside the door, careful not to get noticed again. Her room was diagonally across the living room. The strange young man had disappeared so she pushed the door out some more, increasing her vantage point. The young man was now seated on the couch across from her brother. He had a Beatles haircut, wheatish complexion and a boyish smile. His socks had tiny giraffes printed on them.

Cute! She thought. She looked to the entrance and saw his rain boots neatly parked with the rest of the shoes.

The man was holding some sort of heavy, metallic object that appeared to be the shape of a little human. He placed it on the coffee table for her brother to see.

'What's up, bro? How have you been?' Akash reached out to give the man a hug.

'We just talked in the game *literally* four hours ago!' the man retorted.

'*Arre!* Do you call meeting in a game, "meeting"?' Akash asked plainly.

'Considering we play every day! Yes,' quipped the man.

'So tell me, how's the prototype coming along?' Akash continued, changing the subject.

'Okay, so here it is,' the man said pointing towards the metal object. 'I've been making some progress but now, just some of the software part is remaining. I wish Gautam and Salman were here, their programming expertise could come in handy,'

'No problem, bro. As long as the project has some real value, we can call them down anytime,' said Akash.

'Must be Akash's friend from IIT,' Saloni speculated.

'So I'm thinking of naming this robot, *Bawarchi*,' the man continued.

Saloni was confused. *Who names a robot, Bawarchi? He's probably a dork from IIT.* She thought as she continued to spy on them.

'Okay, watch this!' the man said, now completely focusing his attention to the metal object on the coffee table.

Akash's fingers formed a V-shape holding his chin, his eyes fixated on the robot.

The man opened the top of the robot's head compartment. He appeared to be inserting in some ingredients, what looked like semolina, followed by some spices. The robot let out a loud whirr for a couple minutes. After the sound died down, the man inserted a bowl in the robot's 'stomach area'. The robot started dropping out some sort of mixture into the bowl.

Saloni was horrified. *WTF is this! Is he going to poison my brother?* She considered intervening, but then decided to wait.

'Piping hot upma is ready, sir! Courtesy your very own personal *Bawarchi*!' gleamed the man. He was beaming with joy.

Saloni's jaw dropped. She couldn't tell if this man was a genius or a psycho.

'Holy Shit!' exclaimed Akash. He took a deep breath, inhaling the aroma. Then, they both grabbed a spoon lying by the table and started eating the upma.

'This is so freaking good!' gasped Akash. He high-fived the man.

'So what else can it make?'

'Arre bro, the menu is limited to idli, upma, and poha at the moment. Hence the help of the software guys is needed,' replied the man. He sounded slightly concerned.

'That sounds great but there's one problem,' said Akash.

'What?' asked the man inquisitively.

'If we want to release Bawarchi in the market, then what will happen to our home chefs, like Bablu?'

Akash raised his eyebrows and raised his palms up to face the ceiling gesturing his question.

'Hmm good question, why don't we ask him?' said the man.

'Good idea. Oye Bablu! Come to the hall!' screamed Akash.

Saloni observed Bablu emerge from the kitchen, armed with a spatula. He was a short, lanky young man with a toothy grin. He was wearing a green t-shirt, brown shorts and a red and white checkered apron dangled around his neck. He looked at the man seated next to Akash and smiled.

'Arre Rishabh bhaiya!'

Hmm Rishabh, thought Saloni. *Nice name*.

'Hi Bablu, so we've created a robot named Bawarchi, meaning chef. Its role is to make food, similar to how you do. It has just made some upma, would you like to try?' explained Rishabh.

Bablu looked uncertain. He set his hands on his hips with the spatula behind his back.

Can't blame him, thought Saloni. *This thing looks sketchy!*

'Sure! okay,' said Bablu, with hesitation.

Rishabh did another demo and handed a fresh bowl to Bablu.

'Bhaiya, is the masterchef Sanjeev Kapoor hiding somewhere in this machine?' Bablu asked with genuine curiosity.

Rishabh and Akash chuckled as Bablu took a spoonful of the upma.

'The spice levels are slightly low for my liking, but the overall flavor is pretty good. What is this thing bhaiya?' he asked.

Two people have given their stamp of approval now. Saloni had started to change her mind about this robot.

Bablu was whirling around the table as if taking *parikramas* around it. He was observing the robot like a dog observing a cat for the first time. He strayed away from touching it though.

'We call this a robot. A machine that saves us time in daily tasks,' explained Rishabh.

'The important question is, if we were to keep a machine like this at home, would that concern you about the security of your job?' Akash sounded genuinely curious.

'How will the robot set the menu or the table? Does it know you like to eat eggs and that Saloni didi prefers Bhindi? There needs to be someone with actual brains who can strategically advise it. In a way it's good, I'll get to be its boss, Bablu Sir,' he replied confidently with a big smile plastered across his face.

The boys erupted in laughter. Saloni too let out a quiet giggle, careful not to reveal her presence.

'In either case, if this is around I'll have more time to play BOA,' Babu continued.

'Slacker! When did you start playing BOA?'Akash raised his hands, and slapped the air comically.

'Yup, I'm a top player. I'm already at Mocassin Assassin level 5,' Bablu declared with pride.

'What! How?! That's even higher up than us! How about a game then? The bean bag's open for you,' Rishabh said.

Bablu hesitated.

Akash got up and tapped Bablu's back gently. 'Hey Bablu, you can play with us anytime, no reason for any hesitation or awkwardness,'

'But if I catch you playing during work hours, you better watch it!' Akash teased.

'I'll just block you, then there's no way you can catch me online,' Bablu let out a shy giggle.

'Bro, you're always getting burnt, even at the hands of Bablu!' Rishabh laughed.

Saloni was still observing. She had never thought her brother could be capable of compassion but this warm gesture towards their cook comforted her.

It must be Rishabh's influence, she thought. She shifted her gaze back to Rishabh.

The three boys pulled out their mobiles.

Oh god, this BOA epidemic resumes! Thought Saloni as she rolled her eyes. She remembered her friends in Kolkata, complaining about their boyfriends being hooked to the game.

'What's your username?' Rishabh asked Bablu.

'It's "BhayankarBablu", one word,'

The boys laughed hard this time. Saloni couldn't control herself either. She let out a piercing guffaw. On realizing that she had been caught, she hurriedly retreated to her room and shut the door, her back pressed against it.

She jumped as she heard a knock.

'Are you trying to be Sherlock Holmes? Come out and meet Rishabh,' Akash said nonchalantly.

Saloni followed dutifully, her head lowered in guilt.

'Rishabh, meet my little sister, Saloni. She just moved here from Kolkata a couple days ago. Saloni, meet Rishabh Kulkarni, one of my closest friends from IIT,'

Rishabh stood up to shake her hand. Saloni smiled sheepishly.

'Hi, I'm Saloni,' she said, taking his hand.

'So, what brings you to Mumbai?' Rishabh asked.

'Economics at Sophia College,' Akash interjected.

Rishabh turned to Akash and asked, 'She can speak, right? Let her talk!'

Love the confidence! Saloni thought to herself smiling at Rishabh.

'What he said,' Saloni responded.

'That sounds cool,' said Rishabh.

'As you already know, we studied mechanical engineering at IIT,' he added, gesturing towards Akash and himself.

'Of course, show-offs,' Saloni quipped.

Rishabh chuckled.

'Well, it was nice meeting you. I'm sure we'll keep bumping into each other. If you need anything feel free to let me know,' said Rishabh.

'Well, there is something actually,' Saloni said in all seriousness.

'Oh sure! What's up?' His face turned serious too.

'I was wondering if you could tutor me? I've never lived outside Kolkata before so taking a couple days to adjust here. I don't want my academics to suffer though,' Saloni said.

'Only on quant subjects of course,' she added quickly. She didn't want to sound too suspicious.

Rishabh paused for a second and appeared to be in thought.

'But you have an IIT graduate right here in your home, why not ask him?' he said pointing at Akash.

'Have you met him? His arms are bigger than his brain,' she said, forming a narrow shape with her fingers to prove her point.

Whoa where'd this confidence come from? She felt impressed with herself.

Rishabh laughed.

'She has a point, Akash. Bro what's happening? First Brown Swan, then Bablu and now Saloni. Burn after burn after burn! I'd recommend a cold shower after this,' he teased Akash with barely-contained amusement.

Akash quickly went red in the face.

'I'll be happy to teach you. When do you want to start? I work weekdays so it would need to be after 7.30 p.m.,' he said.

'How about Tuesday at 7.30 p.m.?' she asked.

'Sure!'

'Okay see you then,' she said, almost instantly turning her back towards them.

❖

When she reached her room and shut the door, she pushed her fist up in the air and jumped in excitement. Her heart pounded as she smiled to herself.

Wait! Who's Brown Swan? she pondered.

5
Riddle me this

Rishabh whistled to the entrance of his apartment and rang the doorbell. His mom answered the door. He waltzed his way in the entry passageway whilst balancing the weight of the robot in his arms buoyantly.

'What's going on?' his mom asked quizzically.

He spun around again and circled his mom, almost engulfing her in his strange dance moves. He flew the robot around her head while humming a made-up tune. His mom dodged the swings of the robot carefully.

'What's with the excitement? Did you meet a girl?' his dad chimed in.

Rishabh almost dropped the robot on the floor.

'What? No! I'm just excited about my robot. Akash loved it,'

Rishabh set the robot on the dining table and proceeded to toss a pillow in his father's direction.

'Oh! Come on, dad! You know how hard I have worked on this,'

'So what did it do today, Rishabh?'

'It made upma! By the way I decided on a name, presenting Bawarchi!' Rishabh gleamed with pride. He gestured towards the robot like a magician presenting his latest trick.

'Oh wow! So can I give Shanta the day off tomorrow? Is this our new personal chef?' asked his mom.

Rishabh rubbed his hands together before fielding the question.

'Not just yet, it still needs work on the software side. I want it to be versatile so it can prepare a variety of recipes, but for now, I'm focusing on a simple menu for the single, unmarried professional's survival. I also need to work on any glitches so it doesn't harm anyone,'

'Ah, here I was thinking it's a reincarnation of Dr Evil,' smirked his dad.

'On a more serious note, what if someone tries to hack it and use it as a tool for sabotage? When you're dealing with food you're directly liable for your consumers' health,' his dad added.

'Exactly! Which is why I plan to put some tamper controls in place. It's difficult to fully avoid hacks these days but I can set awareness scenarios such that if there's any hint of malfunction, the robot self-destructs – not by exploding but by shutting down completely. The user can then return it to us for a refund so we can investigate the issue,' responded Rishabh.

'Hmm… seems like you have thought through the minute details as well. Good work, I'm proud of you,' he continued while patting Rishabh's back.

'Yeah, I've spent the last three years toiling on this project. It's got my blood, sweat and tears, literally. It's my baby. Thank you both for supporting me through my dream project. I couldn't have done it without you two,'

'It's all you son, we're just here to support you.'

'Oh by the way, I forgot to mention, Akash wants to help fund this project. He's offered to take care of production, marketing and launch costs,'

His father frowned.

'And how much equity does he want in return?' he asked.

'We haven't discussed it yet, but probably 25%,'

'OK please be careful,' his dad warned.

'Oh, why do you say so? He's my best friend, I trust him, dad,'

'Yes but Akash doesn't have money right now which means Goenka will own 25% of your company in the infancy stage. All I'm saying is be careful and let's work through the best deal. I'd hate to see your first project in trouble before it even takes off. Just like you need safeguards in engineering practices, you need legal safeguards in business too. Let's get the work on your patents started immediately,' his dad explained.

Rishabh's dad, Mr Manoj Kulkarni, was a sought after corporate attorney. He was a humble man though; his main vice was failing to be a people pleaser, unlike his counterparts in the firm. As a result, he often got overshadowed by younger colleagues who had the gift of gab and a penchant for winning clients through flattery. Knowing his son had similar traits, Mr Kulkarni grabbed every opportunity to warn Rishabh, lest he may suffer the same injustices in his career as well.

'Okay, thanks dad. See, this is exactly why I need you,' said Rishabh with a soft smile. 'Alright I'm going to turn in, I've got work tomorrow. Good night guys,' he called out, retreating to his room.

He changed into his casual track pants, t-shirts and slipped under his cozy, striped sheets. The sliding windows were open, inviting a soft breeze which caressed his face. The rain had ceased, leaving a clear cast sky with twinkling stars and a crescent moon.

It was a good day. Akash and his sister are cool. I hope I remember whatever I need to tutor her on. I should probably text her tomorrow so I can prepare,

Brown Swan was fun too. Should I check if she's online? Or is that too desperate? It's 11.30 p.m. here so could be 11a.m. where she is. Let's just check.

He reached for his cellphone and its light projected a glow on his rested face.

On the BOA app, he opened his friends list. Jagger online, Annihilator online, where's Brown Swan… he scanned quickly. "xxBrownSwanxx offline", it read.

'*Ah no worries*,' he thought. He proceeded to start a game with a random squad he got matched with and got busy with it. In the midst of an intense battle in the highly trafficked *Mamba Droga* area on the Góra map, a message flashed in the corner of his phone screen. Rishabh paused his gameplay to check it.

xxBrownSwanxx: Yo! Game?

He hurriedly apologized to his teammates and exited the game.

xxBrownSwanxx is inviting you to join a team.

Rishabh accepted and her familiar avatar appeared on the screen next to his. It waved at him.

'You didn't have to leave your game!' she said.

'It's okay. It was just with randoms,' he replied assuringly.

'Ah! Okay cool, I'm inviting someone, hold on,' she said.

'Okay,' he responded, slightly dejected.

LeeopardKing123456 joined the team.

Jeez people have the weirdest names, Rishabh thought.

'Hello hello! Anyone have a mic?' said an excited, squeaky voice. He sounded South African and his voice wasn't cracked so Rishabh guessed he was probably around eleven or twelve years.

'Yes,' they responded in unison.

'Hey Swan, you want to see the skins I unlocked today?' he asked excitedly.

'Sure,' she responded.

A virtual fashion show ensued, with LeopardKing showing them the slick, fancy outfits he'd just acquired.

'Who's Kraken, Swan? Can we kick him off the team?' LeopardKing said angrily.

'Let's just start the game,' she replied, diffusing the situation.

As the game loaded, Rishabh took the opportunity to ask, 'So what are the plans, Swan? Should be early there right? You bright eyed and buddy tailed?'

'Prepping for work, I guess,' she replied.

'Work? How old are you, Swan?' LeopardKing asked in a concerned tone.

She paused for a second, leaving Rishabh confused.

So mysterious

'I'm fifty,'

Rishabh's jaw dropped.

'Fifty?!' replied Leopard.

'Did you hear fifty? It's fifteen actually,'

Oh god that's even worse

'Just kidding, what do you care about my age, man! How old are you?' she added.

'Oh I'm twelve,' he said.

'I would be careful if I were you! I could even be your mom from the next room,' she said earnestly.

'Let's just play,' grumbled LeopardKing.

'Haha chill man I'm just messing with you. I'm not your mom and I'm twenty-six actually,'

Rishabh's face lit up. Maybe he could talk to her after all.

'What's your name? My name's Rishabh,' he said.

She paused again.

'I'm Sam,'

'Sam?' he responded quizzically. 'Isn't that a dude's name?'

She laughed.

'You decide bro, Sam or Swan? Take your pick!'

Rishabh was intrigued.

Before he could ask another question, the game ended, with them all getting killed pretty quickly.

'That was fun! See you later,' she said, signing off.

Seconds later she was offline.

Here's a riddle I'd love to solve, thought Rishabh tossing his phone to the side.

6
Samira

4.30 a.m. Los Angeles, CA

Powerful winds collided against the windows of a quaint apartment in West Hollywood. The glass cackled with force and struggled to hold its own. The inhabitant of the apartment tossed and turned in her queen size bed. A few seconds later, she was awake.

'Ha!' she gasped. Her heart pounded and her feet tapped furiously but the expression on her face remained blank. Her long, black tresses were disheveled and her black Led Zeppelin t-shirt was crumpled. Still half asleep, she felt delusional.

The same dream again. A familiar man strangling her.

What time is it? She wondered as she reached for her cellphone. The harsh light disturbed her tired eyes as she resorted to squinting. Five missed calls and seven text messages from Sahil. She let out a groan but her facial expression stayed still. She tossed the phone back nonchalantly without checking its contents.

'I have to be up in a few hours,' she mumbled.

Her throat was parched and she guzzled some water. She then reached for the half smoked joint on her nightstand and placed it between her luscious lips.

Hopefully the second half of this will do the trick.

Her black nail polish chipped away with the lighter's embers. She lay back down blowing smoke rings at the ceiling. As they cleared out, a giant poster of Jim Morrison stared back at her. She smiled weakly and said,

'Thank god for you, Jim,'

A minute later she was sound asleep.

❖

6.30 a.m.

The shrill alarm interrupted her slumber.

'Screw you,' she mumbled knocking the phone over. It toppled to the floor.

She sluggishly dragged her feet to the vanity mirror of her bathroom and stared at herself. Her long black hair was tangled and there were bags under her eyes.

'Jeez I look like Samara from *The Ring*,' she said in disgust.

She yawned and stretched, revealing the outline of a lion tattoo on her left bicep. His mane was starting to fade. She stroked it for a second.

Where did I go wrong? Why is my self-confidence in the toilet?

Voices began to haunt her.

'Good girls don't get tattoos,'

'What are you? Some sort of vagabond?'

Why do I suddenly care about this?

She scrunched her brows and shook her head in disappointment.

Fuck that shit!

Sam brushed her teeth, put on activewear and went on a five-mile run to clear her head. Back home, she showered and quickly did her makeup. After a blow dry, she detangled her hair and let it cascade down her shoulders like a smooth waterfall. She rimmed her eyes with kohl, expertly camouflaging the bags. Then, she put on a pink striped shirt, a grey pencil skirt and slipped a matching grey blazer around her shoulders. She completed the look with gold earrings and light red lipstick. Her hair was finally up in a neat bun and her black embroidered heels were fastened on.

Beauty is a façade.

She requested an uber to Century City, the financial hub of Los Angeles. A few minutes later, a grey Prius arrived in her driveway. "Cesar, five stars", read the app.

Five stars? Great! Maybe he'll let me smoke in the car

She slid in as the driver tried to engage in small talk. Sam remained unfazed.

'Hi sir, is it okay for me to smoke? I'll keep the windows open,' she interrupted him.

'Um… sure ma'am,' he hesitated.

She pulled out her American Spirits and cupped her face to light the cigarette.

In the rear view mirror, she observed how the driver's eyes was fixated on her intently. She stared right back making eye contact without blinking, thereby forcing him to look away. She rolled down the glass window and exhaled toxic fumes into the atmosphere whilst grabbing her phone. The same five missed calls and seven messages invited her engagement but she ignored them yet again and opened up the BOA app.

The welcome screen opened up and she immediately received a game invitation from El Padron. She ignored it but noticed a message waiting for her. Message from Kraken

What do you call a BOA addict when he gets diarrhea?

Battle Of Fartsov

She giggled and responded.

xxBrownSwanxx: Haha you're such a dork.
Kraken: Game?
xxBrownSwanxx: Not now. 11.00 a.m. my time?
Kraken: See you then. It may be Navratri right now but winner winner chicken dinner, baby!

She smiled to herself. Gaming might be an escape but she yearned for moments like these wherein she felt comforted.

❖

The Prius came to a halt at the entrance of a skyscraper. Century City was one of the two areas in Los Angeles where skyscrapers existed. It looked like a spotless house of cards made of glass.

The automatic doors slid open as her heels clinked on the Italian marble floors. She waved to the concierge and proceeded to board the elevator.

Kraken seems sweet. What was his name again? Rishabh. Poor guy, I might need to stop messing with him.

But wait, he sent me a message about Navratri. How does he know I'm Gujarati? Did I tell him that? No, I didn't. Did he find a way to stalk me somehow? Am I overthinking about this?

Oh god, I hope this isn't like the last time I opened up to someone online!

The elevator's ding interrupted her anxious thoughts. Her smile faded as she stepped out to the twenty-first floor office of T. Mcdowell Investments.

A cheery smile welcomed her.

'Good morning Sam!'

It was Eric, the office receptionist. He was wearing a grey suit and blue shirt paired with a polka-dotted tie.

'Cute tie, sexy boy!' she shot back.

'Thanks honey,' he responded and puckered his lips.

'By the way, Sahil's looking for you. He says it's about the Boston client,'

'Of course, it is,' Sam responded pursing her lips. 'Thanks, babe,'

The office was an open floor plan – an evolution from the cubicle days. There was a greater social element to it, brought in at the cost of privacy. There were white noise machines installed at regular intervals across the floor to drown out the conversations and enhance focus whilst working. The desks were pristine white and chairs were black with a matte silver finish. They were said to be ergonomic, but for the amount of time that the bankers spent there, it didn't seem to cut it.

Sam approached her desk briskly. She was part of a specialised team of five, presided by her boss – Alex Thompson. Alex was the VP, a respectable man who was in his fifties. His hair and beard were almost entirely silver and always slicked back neatly. He was known as the silver fox, famous for enabling multi-million dollar growth for his clients.

Sam was the token woman on the team. As she sat down, she overheard her team in conversation about work, totally ignoring her presence.

'Have you been monitoring the options on oil prices, Sam?'

'Yep, and I'm keeping an eye on crypto as well,' Sam started her computer and began typing when a firm voice interrupted her.

'Miss Samira Patel, thank you for gracing us with your presence,'

She could hear her colleagues laugh in hushed tones. Then, she closed her eyes and took a deep breath in disbelief before turning around.

A six-feet tall man in a tan, double-breasted suit entered her peripheral vision. His dark hair was neatly parted and his clean-shaven face made his square jaw more prominent. He wore rimless glasses and his hands were in his pockets as he addressed her.

'Hi Sahil. I'm here every day during the week,'

'Ohhhhh,' went her colleagues, in a mocking tone.

'Our Boston client, Apollo Constructions, runs on eastern time, three hours ahead. Which means you need to be here at 6.00 a.m., which would be 9.00 a.m. their time,' sneered Sahil.

Condescending chuckles erupted again. Sam shot her teammates a death stare, making them look away immediately.

'Anyway, it's okay. Step into my office for a second?' Sahil continued with a curt smile plastered on his face.

I wish I could wipe that smile off his smug face.

❖

Sam obediently followed him into his glass-walled cabin and seated herself. She caught people passing by half-smiling at her, probably judging her. She decided to ignore them.

'I hope you left your phone at your desk. You know the rules,' began Sahil.

'Yes, I did,' she mumbled. 'It's not like the whole office doesn't know about us though,' she added with contempt.

'Samira, how many times do I need to explain this to you? I love you, but to maintain the sanctity of our relationship, I can't risk anything! There are only two simple rules for you to follow. Keep your phone away from our interactions and when I'm not with you, *always* answer my calls and messages, whatever the time. How hard is that to do?'

Samira crinkled her brows and her lips quivered.

"Sanctity of our relationship?" It's far from holy. You say you love me but instead you hold me captive. You're afraid of the #MeToo *movement so you even have me keep my phone away in case I'm recording. You're a coward Sahil Arora.*

She curled up her fists tight in her lap to weigh each thought. She couldn't risk creating a scene here, so she had to control herself. Instead she said, 'I don't know what you're so afraid of Sahil. I was actually attracted to you the first time we met at Honor Bar two years ago. I'm not sure…'

'Was attracted?' he said, cutting her off, with that smug smile back on his face. His eyes were dancing more crazily than ever.

Anyway, I forgive you,' he continued, sliding his hand across her thigh from under the table.

She flinched reflexively. 'You're not afraid of the cameras in the office now?'

His crazy eyes widened.

'Ha!' he exclaimed. 'I set the rules. Ma'am, so obviously I'm aware of every nook and cranny that falls in the vision of the camera. We're okay, don't worry,' he grabbed her thigh tighter.

She cringed and rolled her eyes.

'So, I'd like you to come over tonight, around 9.00 p.m. I'm cooking Cacio e pepe, your favourite. Over a bottle of Moet et Chandon.'

'Champagne? What are we celebrating?' Sam felt suddenly disoriented.

'You forgot?!' He tightened his grip on her thigh further. 'It's our two-year anniversary!' he gleamed excitedly.

'So, I'll see you at 8? You'll have no excuses because I've already spoken to Alex about us going to a "client dinner".'

'Of course,' she said half smiling. 'Can I go now?'

'Onward!' he said cheerfully, letting go of her leg which had gone sore.

Samira's face muscles tightened as she exited his cabin. Her jaw clenched and heart raced in fury. Her eyes moved swiftly from left to right and her pulse quickened as she grew anxious with her state of hopelessness.

Was that really her inside? That petrified, subjugated lamb?

She rushed back to her desk, ignoring the snarky comments from her teammates. Before she has a second to decompress, her phone rang.

It was her mom. She hastily answered it.

'Hello?'

'Samira beta! *Su thayu*? Why aren't you answering my calls?' she sounded worried.

'I'm at work, mom,' she said, rising from her chair to find a private corner to talk. She headed to the stairway to continue the conversation.

'Okay listen, I signed up for a matrimonial site,'

'Why?' Samira was genuinely confused. 'Last I checked you and papa were still married?'

'*Ullu ki patthi*, it's for you!'

'Me? I'm just twenty-six, what's the rush ma?' Samira asked.

'Exactly, you're *twenty-six*! In our times we were all married by twenty-one!'

'It's 2020 mom... times have changed,' she dragged out her response.

'What's the harm in just meeting? I just ask that you meet these boys. If we wait too long all the good ones will be taken!'

We're not going shopping mom.

'In school, we gave you the freedom to do as you pleased right? You played guitar and drums. Beena aunty used to call it the devil's music, still we allowed it. Can't you do this for us now?'

Samira rolled her eyes to the heavens and beyond. *The emotional blackmail continues.*

She was in no mood to fight this, not at the present moment at least.

'Okay fine, mom, go for it,' she gave in.

At least it'll keep her busy for sometime

'Great! So, a boy is coming over this weekend! I told him you'd be around! Can you come home?'

Samira was utterly dumbstruck.

'So, when can we expect you? 12:00 p.m.? You'll drive, no? I'll make your favourite *undhiyu* and *thepla*!'

It's funny how Indian moms just assume.

'Ok sure, mom. See you then,' Samira said in defeat.

She hung up.

I need a smoke.

She made her way up to the roof. There, she lit a cigarette, and gazed at the vast concrete jungle beneath her as her mind wandered off.

How do I break up with Sahil?

❖

Two years ago

Sam was engrossed in her phone, swiping with matches on Hot or Not casually along with her high school friend, Neha.

'Check this out!' Neha plopped down on Sam's bed. They were hanging out in Sam's parents' home in Irvine.

Sam inched closer to Neha to get a good look at her phone. They were looking at a picture of a man with a messy stubble, shirtless with six-pack abs, with a dog by his side. It read, "Mike, 27".

'That looks like a fake profile,' Sam teased. 'Six-pack and a dog? How original!'

'Shut up, Sam!' Neha nudged Sam playfully.

'Look, we just matched! You're just jealous!'

Sam laughed. 'He's all yours sister!'

She sat by her drum set and smashed the cymbals.

'Oh god! Samira! Are you planning to bring the world down!' her mom screamed from downstairs.

The girls laughed heartily at the melodramatic shriek.

'What about you, Sam? Let's see your matches,' Neha said, making a beeline for Sam's phone.

'Hmm, let's see,' Sam responded as she continued the frivolous exercise.

She swiped left on a bunch of pictures until she landed on one profile.

It was an image of a suave young man in a black suit. His hair was slicked back with gel and neatly parted to the side. He had a square jaw and a cigar in one hand. "Sahil A, 34, AVP in Finance", the profile read.

Samira paused to check out his bio.

'Give me a chance to uncover you like I do financial equations. I promise it'll lead to profit,' she read out the profile section and smiled broadly.

'I think I'm going to swipe right on this one,' she said, handing her phone over to her friend.

'What?!' Neha chortled. 'He is *so* not your type! You only date tattooed music band dudes!'

'Yeah, but look how that's ended up! Why not mix it up?' she cocked her eyebrow, biting her thumbnail thoughtfully.

'I mean he's handsome and all, but looks like a total fuckboy. He's also ten years older than you!' Neha argued.

'Hmm! Says the girl swiping right on every dude with a six-pack? He'll probably be more experienced. Besides, I'm due to start at T. Mcdowell in two months. Maybe, he'll teach me a thing or two,' Sam sounded serious as she swiped right. They instantly matched.

'I could never understand you, you're such a weirdo,' Neha gave up, rolling her eyes.

Sam lit a cigarette.

'Yeah my mom calls me "black sheep". But I don't understand why anyone who chooses to have an opinion outside of societal norms either has to be a sheep or an ugly duckling. I'm a rebel with a cause and I'm a beautiful woman with power. Power to stand up for my self. Why should I allow some dumb ideals to define me?'

'Okay so you're more like a Brown Swan then. Rebellious and beautiful!' Neha said wryly.

Sam paused for a second.

'Yes! That's it!' she exclaimed, as if basking in the "Eureka" moment.

❖

A week later Sam was ensconced on a bar stool at Honor Bar in Beverly Hills, Los Angeles. Her long black hair was let down and her strapless, royal blue dress shimmered in the dimmed lights. Her leather jacket lay on the stool next to her.

'Want me to check your coat?' the bartender asked.

'No it's okay, I'm not sure how long I'm staying,' she replied.

A few minutes later she heard a voice behind her.

'Can I buy you a drink?'

It was the suave, suited man from Hot or Not.

He's pretty hot in person!

'Hi, I'm Sam, short for Samira,' she said, rising up to greet him. He hugged her as she felt his strong muscles tighten around her.

'Sahil Arora,' he said.

'So, what can I get you?' he asked, looking her up as they seated themselves.

'Vodka soda would be great!'

He signaled the bartender and ordered her drink and a scotch for himself.

'So, finance company, huh? Which one?' she asked.

'T. Mcdowell, Century City,'

'What! No way!' she exclaimed a little too excitedly. 'I'll be starting there soon, too,'

'Really? Which department?'

'Risk. You?'

'Investment banking, ' Sahil replied.

'Show off,' she responded with a shy smile as Sahil smirked.

Their drinks arrived and they clinked their glasses, taking in the booze and the view seated across from them. Sam stared straight into his eyes, unflinching as she took a couple sips of her vodka soda.

The conversation of the people seated at the table adjacent to theirs heated up.

'What would you like honey?' the man asked.

'I was reading, dumbass! Can't you wait a second,' the woman replied, taking her head out of her phone.

'Chill out! I was just asking,'

'Don't ever tell a woman to chill out! I was in the middle of a sentence and you interrupted me,' she almost screamed.

Sam and Sahil giggled awkwardly.

'Would you rather want to shift tables?' he asked courteously.

'No! Let's stay, it's entertaining,' she winked with a playful smile. Sahil leaned his glass towards her in agreement and smiled back.

'Okay. Let's play "never have I ever"? It's a different way to know each other. What do you say?' he rolled up his sleeves, as if preparing himself for a challenge.

'Are you trying to get me drunk?" Sam said, narrowing her eyes, a hint of a smile playing at her lips. Sahil's eyes fell on her lips as he smacked his own and looked up to meet her eyes.

'Well, we can always play with water, if you like,' he winked.

'Haha! Touche! Let's do it!'

'Never have I ever voted,' she began.

'What! You're a terrible citizen, I'll ask about why later,' he responded, while taking a swig of his scotch.

'Never have I ever gone skydiving,' he continued.

Sam took a sip of her vodka then interjected, 'never have I ever dated a finance nerd'.

'Never have I ever been truly mesmerized on a first date,' he said.

'What a cliché *and* a lie!' She exclaimed with a big smile.

'I'm serious!' he protested.

'What about the girls from the club? You're a finance dude, man!'

'That's not a first date!' He said half matter-of-factly and half chuckling.

'What? That's cheating, Mr Arora,' Sam declared loudly. 'Drink up!'

'Are you trying to get me drunk?' he teased, doubling down his intake, keeping his eyes on her the whole time.

They paused for a second to take a sip of water. Sahil inched closer and gazed into Sam's eyes. Sam felt excited but she couldn't tell if it was the effect of the alcohol or her attraction to Sahil.

Sahil continued, 'Never have I ever hooked up with someone in a public place'.

Sam raised her eyebrows.

Really! Now?

The next moment they were in the ladies bathroom ripping at each other.

❖

When they exited and got back to the bar, the bartender asked if they wanted replenishments.

'Yes please. This round's on me,' Sam did her best to catch her breath.

'What? Absolutely not!' Sahil handed the bartender his black Amex card.

He reached for her leather jacket that lay intact on the stool next to him and draped it over her shoulders.

'Thanks!' she said.

'Can I give you a ride home?' he asked, putting his wallet back in his breast pocket.

'Dude! I'm not taking you home,' she said.

'Chill! I just want to make sure you get home safe!' He sounded unexpectedly collected and confident.

'Did you not hear the lady next to us earlier? Never tell a woman to chill,' she quipped. They laughed.

Samira was pleasantly surprised at how breezily the next few months went by. She saw Sahil regularly, over several dates filled with expensive champagne, international cuisine, leisure travels, all peppered with a healthy exchange of invigorating ideas and romance. She met his friends, got formally introduced to his mother and even accompanied him on a trip to Berlin when he went there for business.

Within three months of dating, Sahil had asked her to be his "girlfriend".

When Sam informed Neha, she was equally shocked.

'Unbelievable,' was Neha's exact response.

'I know right?' Sam replied hysterically. 'Sahil and I have been discussing finance too. He's trying to shift me over to the investment banking department,'

'But Sam, you don't even like finance. You only got into it for your dad, or so I thought," Neha trailed off seeing Sam's expression alter.

'Yeah I know, but now that I'm in it I might as well try to make the most of it right? Sahil has really made me see the good in it.'

'I don't know why, but this Sahil seems shady. Just trust your instincts, please,' Neha warned her. Sam shook it off, 'you're being too paranoid. He's not bad actually'.

Sahil was able to get her into a specialized team under Alex Thompson within the next month. Taking his advice she even made recommendations to the client on certain significant investments.

Things were going well, until on their six-month anniversary, the day he asked her to move in with him.

'Aren't we moving too fast?' she asked hesitantly.

'Fast? We love each other, right? If it's now or after a year, what difference does it make?' he said as he wrapped her in his arms.

'It does to me, I'd rather wait,' she said, releasing herself from his grip. She could not breathe around him. And then, she saw a side to him that she'd never seen before.

His head bowed down for a second and when it rose back up, his eyes were narrow and laced with unmistakable fury.

'So, you're going to defy me?'

She was taken aback.

'What the hell is wrong with you, Sahil?'

'What's wrong with me?' She could see his palms curl into stony fists. He looked at her – a calm look on his face, but his eyes were turning red now.

'You know those investments you made? They were all in shady companies and since *you* were the one who recommended them to the client, I went ahead with them and supported you. But if something were to go wrong, there could be serious consequences. The company has already lost a million dollars because of your stupid investments, but I saved your ass. And only I can protect you from it all, as long as you *listen* to me!

He paused and took a giant step towards her. She flinched, and that seemed to annoy him further. He smirked and continued, 'So now the ball is in your court'.

'You don't have to move in with me, but if you care about your job, you'll have to follow *my* rules. Do you understand, *Samira*?'

'So you essentially want me to be your bitch, Sahil?'

Sahil fixed his gaze on a wall. He rose up slowly from the living room and slammed the door to his bedroom behind him.

❖

Back in the present moment, Sam was so lost in thought on the rooftop that she didn't realize when her cigarette burnt her finger.

'Ouch,' she flinched.

She checked her phone, it was 11.05 a.m.

Oh wait I was supposed to play a game with Kraken. Shooting stuff might be a good option right now!

She opened the BOA app with its serpent icon and found him online, waiting for her.

'Hey Kraken, up for a game?'

'Hey sure, and call me Rishabh,' he responded jovially.

'Oh right! Rishabh,' she sounded a bit weary.

They started a game and continued the conversation over voice chat.

'Am I allowed to ask if you're okay?' Rishabh's voice was laced with concern.

'Yeah! I guess! Don't worry about it.' She shook her head slightly as if to clear the fog that had settled upon it.

'Hey, I know you don't know me at all and you don't have to divulge any details, but I'm a mean problem solver,' Rishabh tried to uplift the mood, sensing Sam's dejected spirits.

'Really? Okay! How do you approach a problem then?' She was genuinely curious.

'Okay, fair point! Let's try this again. When your computer has a virus what do you do?'

'I take it to an IT person?'

'Okay, and what does the person do to fix it?'

'Most likely run an antivirus program...'

'Exactly my point!" He exclaimed. 'There's most likely a solution to every problem! You just need to invest some effort to figure out the antivirus,'

Rishabh's pep talk, unbeknownst to him, had reignited her innate feistiness. Something she felt like she had lost ever since Sahil walked into her life.

7
Rag Doll

8.00 p.m. rolled by and Sam stood in the porch entrance of a posh condo in Brentwood. She noticed a package waiting outside and kicked it. It toppled over.

As she walked in, with the package in hand, her sandal-laden feet touched a trail of rose petals.

Oh god, this is a bit out of the ordinary, even for Sahil.

She followed the trail of fresh petals to the living room. It ended at an elaborate set up of a decorated table for two, brimming with fancy delicacies, champagne, chocolates and giant roses.

'There she is!' screamed a voice from behind her that made Sam jump.

'Hey, you scared me there!'

'Happy anniversary, doll!' Sahil said as he lifted her up and down in his arms. The package almost dropped from her hands.

'What's in the package, Sahil? Is it an anniversary gift for me?'

Sam flinched. 'No! It's actually from your mom, I think. I found it by the entrance while walking in,'

'Oh nice! She wanted to congratulate me!'

'Congratulate you? For what?' Sam was suspicious.

Sahil paused, then gave in. 'You ask so many questions! It's like you're my nagging wife already,' he said as he pinched her cheeks.

Sam shuddered. 'No seriously, why is *she* congratulating you?'

'Because we just completed two years, silly! I'm getting old now so it means something to her for me to have a serious partner,'

Sahil was dressed in a tuxedo. Sam was just beginning to notice this.

'Why are you so dressed up, you weirdo?' she said, chuckling awkwardly, hoping she hadn't given away her fears.

'I like to get dressed up for you! Now come on! No more questions. I'm in a good mood and I have things planned.' He kissed her cheek. Her eyes wavered from side to side.

'So, let's see what my mom has sent,' he said, relieving Sam's tight grip around the package.

He slowly pulled out a swan figurine and began examining it.

'Hmm this is odd! Why would she send a swan? Should I call my mom and ask her about the swan?' Sahil asked.

Sam let out an audible sigh. Then, she slumped her shoulders and moved towards the couch. She kicked off her heels and sank down. She saw Sahil gazing at her from the corner of her eye with a thoughtful expression. Moments later he approached her again.

'You know what, it's okay, I can call her tomorrow. Besides, this is our special night. The swan is kinda cute too. I'm just going to place it on the shelf for now and then we'll continue right where we left off. Cool?'

Sam simply nodded.

Sahil took her hand and guided her to the table. When they were both seated, he poured out some champagne and handed her a glass. As she reached to take a sip, he stopped her.

'Not yet,' he said.

'What, you're scaring me!' Sam was baffled.

'Scaring you? I just wanted to give you a surprise'

'What's this surprise? It's making me extremely anxious!' She immediately regretted her words.

'Well, since you've ruined the surprise, I bought us tickets to Hawaii, but patience isn't one of your virtues is it?"

Sam closed her eyes. She took a deep breath and a calm smile spread over her face. Sahil raised an eyebrow in suspicion.

'Why do you look so relieved?' Sam looked up and smiled wider.

'It's just... I thought you were going to propose.' She had done it again.

Sahil pushed his chair back and crossed his arms.

'Sahil, can we just have an honest conversation, please? It's taken a lot of courage for me to even bring this up. Look I'm just tired of being your rag doll man.' Sam felt a bit of her old self seep back into her bones.

'What?' Sahil muttered with clenched teeth.

'I'm just tired of your constant ordering me around and domination. "Text me back, keep your phone away, no talking to guys, etc. etc.", it's just so controlling... it makes me wonder whether you actually even want a girlfriend or just a pet dog!' She drew in a deep breath.

Sahil listened intently, one hand in his trouser pocket, the other curled up tight in a fist.

'Okay, go on,' he said, tightening his fist.

'Yeah and this whole thing with the "shady" investments being dangled over my head like a carrot... '

'What about it?' He leaned in closer.

'Well, I didn't have the courage to say it before but you keep holding me hostage for making the investments that you say lost the company a million dollars, but Alex didn't mention it and neither did the client. You are the only person who claims to have seen these numbers, but I haven't seen these figures anywhere. I just don't know what to believe at this point,'

Sam's pulse rate increased as she reached the last part of her rant. She paused to gauge Sahil's reaction but he just stared at her coldly, in complete silence.

Why won't he say anything. Focus Sam, antivirus, antivirus, antivirus, antivirus.

'Is there anything else?' Sahil asked coolly.

'I just said a lot, Sahil and it's kind of fucked up that you won't even react!' Sam was aware she needed to stop now but her self-control was clearly out of the window.

Sahil gulped his champagne and smiled spitefully.

'You've got some nerve coming down here and blabbering your shit,' he unfastened his bow tie.

'When I met you... remember our first date at Honor Bar? It was like you heard the name T.Mcdowell and just got instantly turned on,'

'What the f...,' Sam was about to say something but Sahil raised his hand in front of her face to silence her.

'You're out of turn! It's my turn to speak now. So, as I was saying, all the fancy dates, gifts, expensive business trips you accompanied me on, where were these complaints then? I even got you on Alex's team. Shifted you from the shitty Risk to investment banking – the most coveted and highest paying department! When you fucked up, I backed you up. The reason you don't hear about it is because I swept it under the rug. Finance is complicated, Samira. What do you even fucking know? You're just a maths professor's daughter! You're lucky you're a bit attractive but that'll fade over time too. And then we'll see who'll be paying those botox bills you'll be desperate for, because it definitely won't be me!'

Sam raised her eyebrows and stood up. 'Jeez, I didn't realize I was some piece of property or a pet project that you took on,'

'Where do you think you're going? I'm not finished. Sit the fuck down,' Sahil's voice was stern.

Sam continued walking back to the living room. Sahil rose up, took off his coat and neatly hung it on the chair. Then, he followed Sam.

'I don't owe you shit Sahil. All the things you just said, I didn't realize they were debts I was accumulating. I thought they were things people do for each other in relationships. But the last few months have honestly been a nightmare and I'm done,'

Sahil grabbed her arm forcefully. The weight of his body pushed her down on the couch. He pinned her arms above her head and his breath was hot on her face.

'It's not done till *I say* it's done,'

His grip on her wrists tightened as he thrust his weight harder on her body, crushing her.

Sam was on the verge of hyperventilating.

'Sahil, you're hurting me!' She screamed, wrestling her hands to liberate her from his hold.

Sahil let go of her. She continued to lay on the couch, shivering.

He tossed her heels at her and walked away. The spikes of the heels hit her face.

'Ouch, Sahil, you asshole!' she whimpered as he slammed his bedroom door behind him.

❖

When she got home, she took off her makeup and fancy outfit and hid under an oversized hoodie. She then grabbed her guitar and jammed out to death metal for the next few hours until her body got the best of her, knocking her out.

The harsh rays of the sun disturbed her and she noticed it was past 10.00 a.m.

She picked up her iPhone and saw seventeen text messages and twenty missed calls from Sahil.

'Call me Sam, let's talk about this. Don't be foolish, we can work this out!'

She slid her hand into her purse and grabbed a tiny swan figurine.

'Thanks, swan,' she said, smiling at it.

She then transmitted the footage from the swan's camera and airdropped it to her phone. Then she sent the video clip to Sahil and waited for his reply.

She kept seeing him type a message but stop every few seconds.

It was an hour later that she texted him,

I'll be quitting T. Mcdowell soon, don't bother contacting me ever again. If you do, you'll be hearing from the police.

Bye, douchebag! I would say son of a bitch, but your mum's kinda nice.'

❖

A few days later, Sam opened up her BOA app. Kraken was offline. She'd been looking forward to giving him the news.

I need his number or something, this time difference is killing me

She went to get coffee, checked her phone again but Rishabh was still offline. She played her guitar and checked her phone again after twenty minutes. Rishabh still seemed to be offline. After binge watching an entire Netflix show and almost forgetting to check her phone the entire time, Sam jumped to check the app again.

She opened the game with her fingers crossed this time and squealed when she read the name Kraken. She hit the invite button repeatedly till he accepted to play.

When they connected she let out an extended "Heyyyyy!"

'Whoa, someone's excited! What's going on, Swan? Where have you been the past few days?' Rishabh asked candidly.

Sam's mind was racing. 'Well, I was trying to find an antivirus,'

'Haha, what?' Rishabh sounded genuinely confused.

'An antivirus, silly! Remember, you told me the solution for a virus is an antivirus so I went to find the antivirus, and I did, thanks to you!'

Rishabh giggled as Sam sounded like an overwrought child uttering her tale.

'You're going to need to give me a little more context, dude. Care to elaborate?' Rishabh responded curiously.

'Okay so I was basically in this toxic relationship for two years, and I didn't realize it but somewhere along the way I might've lost my self-confidence somewhere. I got scared and subconsciously began to react out of fear. But then, the other day when you brought up your virus/antivirus theory, it hit a note for me,' she sighed.

'Oh really?' he said, sounding absorbed.

'Yeah, it struck a chord and I was able to muster up the courage to face my problem head on,'

'I'm really happy to hear that my nerdy ass theory came in handy. So, have you broken up with this guy now?' he asked, trying to not sound too creepy.

'Yeah he's out of mind and out of sight! Want to play a game?' she asked.

'Yeah, sure, I mean that's why I came online,' he teased.

When they finally began playing after their bantering, Sam observed a glitch in the game where Rishabh's character's leg looked stretched out like a spider's.

'Dude your character looks hilarious right now,'

'What are you talking about?' Rishabh was clueless as Sam continued to laugh.

'Give me your number. I'll text you a screenshot of this. I swear I won't text you again after this but you have to see this,'

Rishabh laughed and sent her his number. A few seconds later, Rishabh began laughing.

'So where are you from and stuff?' she asked, her curiosity finally piqued.

'I'm from Mumbai, 23, I'm a mechanical engineer by profession. On a side note, I love how we're exchanging ASL (age, sex, location) info through BOA,'

'Ah! Now I get where the virus/antivirus theory comes from,' Sam retorted.

Anyway, thanks for listening to me today. I know it's kind of random but I appreciate you listening,'

'No worries, happy to be there anytime. Can I just ask you one question?'

'What is it?'

'Is your name really "Sam"?'

She laughed and he gave in too.

'Haha yeah! It's short for Samira. Ok I gotta go!'

'Wait what! We just started playing!'

'Bye, Rishabh!' She stressed hard on his name so as to let her leave the game.

8

Meet the Patels

Sam crossed ninety miles per hour down the I-5 freeway. Her military green jeep Cherokee squealed smoothly, causing a smile to appear on her face. The highway was pretty smooth with a clear blue sky over. Her fingers tapped the steering wheel to the tunes of the Ramones.

As she cruised ahead, she noticed a sliver of red and blue lights flashing a hundred meters ahead of her.

I better slow down, no more trouble for me. She thought, placing her foot slowly on the brake pedal, bringing down her speed to 60mph.

'You will reach your destination in thirty minutes,' said the monotonous voice of the GPS.

'So, there's three things to sort out –one, I have to figure out how to break the news about quitting T. Mcdowell; two, find a way to get out of this arranged marriage mess; and three, maybe finally tell them about Sahil, since it's over now. Or maybe not about Sahil, this triple dose will give them a heart attack for sure,' she said to herself.

'Or should call Neha first. I think I should,' she said to herself as she counted the list on her fingers.

She dialed Neha who promptly answered.

'Where have you been, girl?'

'So, I'm actually on the way to Irvine right now a...'

'What??' Neha interrupted Sam's train of thought too loudly.

'Arre, listen *meri maa* I promise I'll tell you everything when I get there, so just hear me out, otherwise every two seconds you'll have questions,'

'Grr... okay weirdo, tell me!' Neha was audibly fuming and trying hard to calm down.

Sam took a deep breath.

'Okay! I broke up with Sahil, finally gathered the courage to speak to the asshole in his own language. Then, I quit my job and now, I'm on my way to an arranged marriage meeting with some *champu* my mom wants me to meet. So, I need to get out of that and on top of all this I need to find a way to break the news of me quitting the great job I had to my parents.' Sam paused to take a breath.

There was silence on both ends of the speaker for a second. Sam stared ahead at the road awkwardly.

'Neha, you there?'

'Sam, do you know what they call a person who asks for advice but never takes it? An Askhole! That's what you are! Didn't I tell you about Sahil and your job?'

'Hey, don't judge, Neha! People make mistakes and the important part is to learn from them, right? There's usually a solution for every problem, like there is an antivirus for a virus,' Sam smiled to herself at that last part.

Neha giggled. '*Antivirus for a virus*? When did you start speaking nerd? LOL, what the heck?'

'A very intelligent person told me that and he's right,' Sam scoffed.

'Wow, it just keeps getting better. Can't wait to hear more about this new "smarty pants" when you get here,' Neha's said calmly.

'Listen, I'm getting there in fifteen minutes. Can you please help me with a plan? I don't want Rajesh and Alka to freak out,' Sam sounded genuinely worried.

'Well, that's going to be hard but let's see. So you never told them about Sahil, right? So I suggest you don't bring that up at the moment, it's not the right time. And about the job, I think if you explained it nicely they'll understand, especially your dad. He's so sweet. Parents don't want children to struggle so they will suggest the best path forward based on their experience. Just try to put yourself in his shoes. He doesn't know anything about the music industry; for him it's an unstable career that will require tons of struggle and in a way he's right. Are you ready to struggle, Sam? It's not going to be a simple bi-weekly paycheck you're used to.'

'Well Neha, I am thinking of tackling the corporate side of the music industry first since I have the experience and slowly introducing my music once I have the contacts,'

'So that's the way you approach it with your parents. If you have a plan they will understand, especially Rajesh uncle. He's a reasonable man. You're going to have to face some fireworks from your mom though, not going to lie!' Neha chuckled.

'Thanks Neha, that really helps,' Sam had visibly calmed down and let out a deep breath.

'Also about this arranged marriage situation! I don't think you have much to worry about. Just be yourself and I'm sure they'll be off running,' Neha retorted.

'Thanks Neha, love you!' Sam said as she pulled the jeep into her parent's driveway.

❖

As Sam unlocked the door to her parents' home, she heard chatter in Gujarati emerging from the living room. She took off her shoes and placed them on the rack by the entrance. As she looked around, she froze with a worried expression etched on her face. Her parents had decorated their house with lights reserved especially for Diwali time each year.

Yeh toh shaadi waala vibe dikh raha hai!

Her lips quivered and her heart skipped a beat but she squared her shoulders and proceeded to the living room. As she entered, she paused for a second to read the room. Her mother looked animated as usual, while her father stayed quiet in a corner with a docile smile on his face, watching his wife taking charge of the situation.

Across from them sat a stern looking woman, her hair neatly tied in a bun, wearing a lavender sari with a zari border. Sam's mom, Alka, was boasting about her daughter's accomplishments and how she had managed to gain a spot within a highly coveted team at T. Mcdowell. The stern lady seemed disinterested. She was flanked on one side by an older, balding man with a thick moustache and on the other by a younger man whose hair stood two inches above his head.

Alright, here's my cue. Sam thought, entering the room.

'*Lo aavi gayi* Sam! So pretty you look! How was the drive?' Alka asked pleasantly, raising her chin, grinning at Sam.

'It was good, ma. Hi everyone,' Sam waved and smiled at everyone in the room. Her mom shot her a death stare.

Samira quickly faced the guests and folded her hands and greeted them with a "Jai Shree Krishna". She cringed for a second as she observed the three guests check her out, but managed to hold on to her smile.

She then reached her hand out in front of the young man and said, 'Hi, I'm Samira'.

He took her hand and said, 'Hi, it's Koonal'.

His smile widened, revealing sparkling white teeth that matched the shine of the diamond stud in his left ear.

'Nice to meet you, Kunal,' she replied, gesturing to him to leave her hand.

'Samira, go get chai and dhokla for aunty and uncle,'

'No chai and dhokla for me,' said aunty, 'I'm on keto at the moment'.

'Oh, no problem aunty! What can I get you instead?'

'Green tea works for me and uncle,'

'I'll take a diet-coke,' Koonal added with a wide smile.

'Koonal, enough with the soda, you should have green tea as well,' his mom responded coldly.

'Okay, mom,' Koonal replied like an obedient child.

'Hey aunty, we have some spicy nuts that will cater to your diet. I used to eat them when I was on keto one summer,'

The lady's face perked up. 'You were on keto?'

'Yeah, my friend Neha and I were following a pretty rigid fitness plan last summer, so I followed the diet and it worked, but honestly. I don't know if I recommend it for the long-term. It's too high fat and too few carbs, you just end up feeling hungrier which is not a good sign. I think we just need to get enough vegetables and fruits in our diets first. I feel like that's more effective than any crash diet out there, you know?'

'I'd love to try some of those nuts you mentioned,' she said, returning a smile.

'Of course, aunty, be right back!'

'You can call me Sharmila,'

'Sure, Sharmila aunty,' Sam nodded and walked towards the kitchen. Her mom followed her. As they reached the kitchen, her mom shook her excitedly.

'I'm so impressed, Samira!' A single dramatic tear parted from her mother's eyes. 'That woman hasn't smiled once in the past hour and you've connected with her in barely five minutes! I'm so proud of you and the way you're handling this. I thought you would be completely against this meeting, but here you are!' Alka beamed like a proud mom.

'Don't jump to conclusions yet, we'll see how it goes but I'm obviously not going to be disrespectful. Well, not unless they are.'

'Trust me, Samira, you won't regret this. Uncle owns a few Burger Haven franchises and Koonal is starting another one!'

Sam suppressed her laugh once again and picked up the tray to take it back to the other Patels.

'Here you go, aunty and uncle,' she said as she handed out the drinks and snacks.

She then retreated to her seat anticipating some more questions.

'So you went to Berkeley?' Sharmila aunty asked.

'Yes, majored in Finance,'

'Samira graduated with a 3.9 GPA,' her mom added as if it was an indispensable detail.

'Well I must say you're in great shape, Samira! What do you do to maintain your figure?'

Sam saw Koonal drooling from the corner of her eye. She smiled back awkwardly.

'Thank you so much for the kind words, aunty. To be honest, I just try to run daily, about five miles, and try to eat healthy, nothing special,'

The other Patels looked at her in wonder.

'Arre Samira is just downplaying it! She used to be a track and field champ in school!'

Sharmila ignored her comment again. Samira felt a twinge of anger inside her. She knew her mom could be a little over-the-top sometimes but this woman's complete lack of respect towards her was inexcusable.

Sharmila turned to Koonal and said, 'Well I like her. You can speak to her if you like,'

Koonal nodded excitedly in agreement. Sharmila then turned to Sam and asked, 'Would you mind showing him around, dear?'

'Of course!' Sam got up briskly, a hand in each pocket of her jeans.

This coincided with the arrival of Neha. She quickly observed the environment, exchanging familiar glances with Sam and decided to converse with the aunties while Sam showed Koonal around. Sam took him to her old room by the attic. He scanned the room carefully.

'You play the drums?' He asked, raising an eyebrow.

'Yeah, and guitar too actually!'

'Oh you like rock music,' he continued, observing the Queen and Led Zeppelin posters on her wall.

'Yup. I like all kinds of music, frankly. What about you?'

'Oh nice. I think rock music is too noisy for me. I listen to Gangsta rap,'

Sam shot him a confused look. 'And your mom's okay with that?' Koonal didn't respond.

'Can I ask you something?' she asked a little too quietly.

'Of course, whatever you like,' he said, sounding serious and stepping towards her.

'Do you find me attractive?'

'I think you're a total bombshell,' Koonal replied after studying her face and body for a long second.

Sam smiled sarcastically. 'Okay, so Kunal, whoops sorry, I mean *Koonal*, hypothetically if we were to get married and I gained a few pounds after, would you still want to be with me?'

Koonal shrugged. 'Well I guess it would depend...'

Sam was fuming internally.

'Come here and show me your hands,' She ordered him.

'Huh?' Koonal sounded confused but true to his nature, obeyed.

She grabbed his left hand and measured the distance between his index finger and thumb with her hands.

'They say there's a correlation between the distance between a man's index finger and thumb and the size of his penis. Based on this logic and seeing your seemingly tiny hands, if I encounter any surprises I reserve the right to change my mind too, right?'

Koonal went white as a sheet. He quickly withdrew his hands from her hold and rushed downstairs to where his family was seated.

The temperature of the room seemed like it had dropped sub zero by the time Sam reached the foot of the stairs. She imagined dramatic opera music playing in the background as she gauged the reactions in the room in slow motion. First, she looked at her parents – her father's expression was statue-like, her mother's jaw had dropped and she shook her head in disbelief.

Sam then moved her attention towards the other Patels. Mr Patel was statue-like too, but Sharmila seemed to shoot lasers out of her eyes. It seemed she was hungry for a slice of Sam's soul. Koonal stayed in his mother's shadow, still shocked from Sam's comment but seeking validation from Sharmila.

Finally Sharmila spoke. 'Quite a brat you've raised Alka-*ben*,' she said pursing her lips, her entire body quivering with anger. 'If we knew we'd be coming here to get insulted we'd never even come! *Itni ashleel baatein karne wali ladki ko kaun milega?* You know what, *aap toh Ben bulaane ke laayak hi nahi ho,'*

Alka joined her hands and bowed her head in embarrassment. "Forgive us Sharmila ben but what happened? What did she say?"

'You don't know what she said?' Sharmila sounded angrier now.

Alka and Rajesh shook their heads, completely oblivious to what had just transpired literally above their heads. Sharmila was indignant but forced herself to speak.

'She said… that Koonal is…,' Sharmila held her hand up making an L-shape with her fingers.

Alka and Rajesh narrowed their eyes, still utterly confused, yet apologetic.

Sharmila yelled. 'She said Koonal's property…' while further animating her hand movements. 'Actually it's so dirty I can't even say it! Your daughter is a rude witch and you're to blame for her upbringing!' She put down her hands dejected, throwing a heated stare towards Sam.

'But, Sharmila ben, we can't really understand what she did. *Kuch toh logic hona chahiye na? Itne bade ilzaam ke peeche?*' said Rajesh.

'*Ji* correct!' Koonal's father joined in, pointing a finger towards the air.

Sharmila was shaking profusely but Koonal somehow held on to her like a leech.

'Why don't I clear this up for everyone?'

Sharmila shot her a death stare, while Koonal looked at her fearfully.

'Wonderful! Mr Koonal said if I gain some weight he would not be interested in me and would leave me. In my experience, guys who act douchey are usually trying to overcompensate for something else, if you know what I mean. So I simply asked him about the size of little Koonal, but clearly it seems to have frightened him,'

'Little Koonal?' asked Alka, still confused.

'Yes, how do you say in Gujarati, *sisna*? *Arre chota chetan*, penis!'

Koonal's father chuckled.

His wife shook him while Koonal deepened his grip on his mom's shoulders, hiding further behind her.

'*Hey Ram*, Samira!' Alka screamed, sinking into the couch.

Rajesh's eyes widened but he simply stood there statuesque.

'And what's wrong with what he said?' Sharmila defended Koonal. 'We clearly specified in the matrimonial ad that we wanted a slim daughter-in-law. You are the insecure one, not my son!'

'Right!' Sam blurted. 'Some double standards you have, selling burgers and following keto diets. *Doosron ke muh mein fast food thoos thoos ke unko mota bana do lekin shaadi.com pe jaake hot sexy bahu order kar do?* What logic is this?!' It was Sam's turn to be furious.

Alka stooped and bowed her head in shame in front of Sharmila, her hands folded in apology, pleading for forgiveness.

Sam was baffled. 'What are you doing mom?'

Alka continued pleading.

'Mom stop it! They're not worth it! This woman has been so rude to you since she got here. Didn't I tell you I would be nice unless they were disrespectful? She didn't bother saying a word to you this whole time even though you've been such a wonderful host.

'Hey, aunty, I know my mom can be a bit melodramatic but she definitely doesn't deserve to be disrespected. You've had all sorts of tantrums and requests since you got here and she's been nothing but hospitable,'

'I think we've heard enough! Forget about future alliances within the Patel community, it's not going to happen for your lot,' Sharmila declared determinedly and turned to leave, grabbing her husband.

I guess I bought myself sometime in the arranged marriage department. Sam thought, feeling slightly relieved at their fortunate departure.

❖

Once the Patels left, Alka sank bank on the couch, her hand covering her forehead in shame. Rajesh was seated next to her, consoling his wife.

'Gosh! Could this day get worse?' she said out loud in despair.

'Actually… while we're at it…' Sam sat down across her parents and observed Neha pick up the popcorn bowl from the corner of her eye.

'I quit my job,'

'What!' her mom screamed loud enough for the neighbours to hear.

'Yeah, but hear me out please!' Sam pleaded.

'I took dad's advice and studied finance because I was unsure of what I wanted to do in life and I know the two of you want nothing but the best for me. But once I started working in investment banking and seeing the nasty side of it, I knew what I definitely didn't want to be doing. It's not just about money; it's about finding satisfaction and joy in your work too. If a job is satisfying it's no longer a job, it's just something you enjoy doing and that's what I want, mom.'

'So you just quit? Do you even have a plan?' Her mom was fighting back tears.

'So you know I've been into music all my life and I really want to thank you for supporting me with that. I want to make music. It's going to be a hard journey ahead but I live in Los Angeles, the capital of the entertainment industry. I know it's going to be a struggle initially but I have a plan for that too. Having a background in finance I'm already in talks with a couple of labels for data analytics jobs. Everyone needs someone who is good with numbers these days. I'll use that as my way to enter and slowly try to promote my music internally. I don't know what the end result will be, but I have to try, that's the only way I'll know, right?'

Her mom was still crying but Rajesh was deep in thought.

Sam shot Neha a worried look. The latter put the popcorn down and chimed in.

'Aunty, uncle, the music scene is thriving at the moment. Streaming services are booming and tour tickets are constantly selling out. Charts are topping globally, even in India! You should've seen the crowd that showed up to see Coldplay in Mumbai a couple years back! Sam is so talented. Just, you give her a chance!'

Alka's head stayed bowed down, shaking from side to side. Rajesh, however, continued to process what he was hearing.

A few moments later her dad said, 'Go ahead and try it! I support you,'

Her mom rose up and retreated to her room, muttering something under her breath.

'Don't worry about her,' her dad said, interpreting her thoughts. 'I'll explain to her, but you're an adult Sam and your plan sounds pretty logical to me. I suggested you join finance because it's a lucrative career but like you said, times are changing and your background in finance can enable you to work in a plethora of jobs. I fully support you. Go after your dreams, if that's what you truly want.'

Sam rushed to hug him. He gave a pleasant smile and left the room.

❖

Once Sam's father was out of sight, Neha turned to her and asked excitedly, 'Okay, so who's this new guy?'

'His name is Kraken,'

Neha grimaced, her face contorting. 'Congratulations, you have now graduated to next-level weird,'

Sam giggled loudly. 'Chill man! It's his gaming name. I met while playing a video game. His real name is Rishabh,'

'Do you realize you're making the same mistake again? You just got out of a relationship with the devil's offspring who you met through Hot or Not, and shockingly, instead of learning from it, you've just moved from Hot or Not to a video game? What is wrong with you, Sam?'

Sam sighed and looked down at the carpeted floor.

'Who is this guy? Have you even seen or met him? Wait, don't answer that, you should not be talking to random strangers on the internet, period!'

She then stopped moving, fell back on the bed, and signaled for Sam to answer.

Sam moved to sit next to Neha and wrapped her arms around her.

'Just hear me out. Can you do that, please?'

Neha nodded her head stubbornly.

'So I started playing this mobile game about seven months ago. It's called BOA - Battle Of Arstov. Initially I just started playing to blow off some steam. While Sahil was fucking my mind, I'd shoot people aimlessly in the game. It just became an escapist avenue for me. The game runs off servers globally so you can play with people across the world.

'So players I'd get matched with would sometimes send friend requests so we could play again without having to get matched but I never thought much about it. But one day I got matched with a group of guys from India and it was kind of fun. They had really trendy squad names.'

'Like Kraken?' Neha asked.

'Yeah! He seemed cool so I sent him a friend request,'

'Can I interrupt and ask a question? What's your name in the game?'

'Brown Swan,'

Neha's jaw dropped. 'Seriously?'

Sam shrugged her shoulders.

Neha laughed out loud. 'You took my joke a bit seriously, ha? Is that what Kraken calls you? Swan?' She winked at Sam.

'Uh... yeah,' Sam blushed a little.

Neha clapped. 'What a cute couple, Kraken and Brown Swan. Love story 2022.'

Sam tossed the goofy stuffed toy back at Neha.

'Eh no couple business and all *haan*!'

'OK, then what is it?' Neha asked, sounding genuinely curious.

'I don't know. You know when you're online dating, it's like a game of hot or not, so vain and superficial! But when you're in a game, it's not meant to be online dating so there's no pressure. You just talk to people about game strategy and whatever else you want. It's like blind dating, you can just be yourself,'

'Right,' Neha mumbled.

'I was able to talk to him about Sahil without the fear of being judged. Also he's a mechanical engineer and really smart.

'Oh, now I get the nerdy references. So how long have you been talking to this kid?'

'A few weeks, I think,'

'And have you seen his face?'

'No, not yet,'

'Well,' said Neha, rising up. 'Don't you want to?'

'Yeah, but I never really thought of it,'

'Why don't you text him right now and ask him to send a picture or just stalk him on Instagram!'

Sam shrugged.

'Be realistic, Sam. Here's this guy halfway across the world with whom you've formed a connection. See, he might be a normal guy but maybe, just see what he looks like to put a face to the name. Even if he just turns out to be a friend, it's always good to know who you're friends with!' Neha said casually.

Sam bit her lip, her gaze focused on a poster on the wall.

'Well I'll leave you with that thought, I have got to head home.'

Once Neha left, Sam climbed out of the window and seated herself on the red tiles on the roof. As she rolled herself a joint, she decompressed and analysed her conversation with Neha.

It's time to unveil myself

9

New Developments

Rishabh opened the BOA app on his phone in his cubicle at Zeus Dental Care. Opening the app had become a frequent activity since he met Swan online. He started reading the messages.

xxBrownSwanxx: Yo Captain! Game? Lots to update you on. Also I think it's time to see each other.
Kraken: See each other??
xxBrownSwanxx: Don't get your hopes up or I'll break your teeth. I just meant I want to see your picture.
Kraken: Break my teeth? That seems aggressive!
xxBrownSwanxx: Can you play or not??
Kraken: I'm tutoring someone tonight.
xxBrownSwanxx: You're a teacher too?
Kraken: Somewhat!
Anyway I can play later in the night around 11.30pm.
xxBrownSwanxx: Sure. What you up to?
Kraken: Just messing with someone in the office.
xxBrownSwanxx: The way I do every day?
Kraken: Of course madam. Alright I've got to hop. See you later tonight.

Around 6.30 p.m., Rishabh left his office in Bandra Kurla complex for Akash's apartment in Worli.

As his taxi sped through the Bandra-Worli sea link, Rishabh attempted to refresh his memory on probability and integration.

What is the probability of Brown Swan being who she says she is?

He laughed at his own joke.

❖

When he arrived at Akash's place, he was surprised to find Saloni alone at home.

'Hi Rishabh,' she said smiling.

She was wearing a pink sundress, casual but still formal with a complementing accessory in her hair.

'Hey Saloni,' he said while looking around inside the house. 'Where's Akash?'

'He's still at work. He said he'd be late,'

Rishabh gulped.

'Everything okay?' Saloni asked, looking perplexed.

'Yeah! Why wouldn't it be?'

'Well, you're still standing in the doorway. Come in!'

Rishabh sauntered in nervously and placed his shoes on the rack.

Saloni looked confused. 'Would you like anything? Tea, coffee, water?'

'No, thanks.' He pressed a gawky smile.

They stared at each other awkwardly for a second.

'Okay, I guess then, meet me in the living room when you're ready?'

He followed her and took a seat at the dining table, reaching for some books.

'You can sit next to me if you want, I won't bite,' she said playfully.

'Oh sure,' said Rishabh, rising up to sit next to her.

'I mean it might be easier for us to study then,' she said.

He opened a book.

'But if you don't stop fidgeting with that weird beyblade toy…,' Saloni continued.

'Huh?' Rishabh was caught off-guard.

'You've been fidgeting with that strange toy ever since you walked in through the doors and have been sweating profusely. Have you seen a ghost? Do I have to scare you to get you out of this trance?' Saloni asked, raising her eyebrows.

Rishabh stared at his left hand and dropped the toy.

They paused for a second and started to laugh.

'Sorry Saloni, I just got awkward since Akash isn't here,'

'Oh wow, *itna sharmeela*? Who's the girl here? I'm flattered, but also curious, do they not teach you guys to talk to girls at IIT?' she said as she continued to laugh.

Rishabh laughed harder.

'Okay, since the awkwardness is behind us, want to study a bit?' Rishabh said, gaining composure.

'Finally,' Saloni laughed again as Rishabh went red in the face.

❖

After they were done studying, Rishabh started to gather his things as Saloni asked Bablu to prepare some tea.

'I should get going actually, but does every Tuesday work?' Rishabh asked as he pulled the strap of his bag over his head and across his shoulder.

'Oh you sure? Bablu just got back, he makes a tasty vada pav,' Saloni insisted.

'I definitely can't say no to a good vada pav,' Rishabh grinned, placing his bag back down on the table.

'Okay then I have a better idea,' she said. 'Let's go take a walk on Sea Face and get vada pav. I'm new here too. Could use some fresh air!'

Rishabh hesitated and scratched his hair.

'Oh, c'mon! I thought we were past that awkwardness,'

Rishabh folded his hands in defeat. 'Okay, you win, Saloni! After you,' he said, allowing her to lead the way.

As they walked down the Sea Face, they stopped for vada pav at a stall.

'Hmm!' uttered Rishabh, taking a large bite. 'I could eat this every day,'

'It's pretty good, but can't beat Calcutta street food. Puchkas and Kathi rolls? To die for!' Saloni groaned.

They continued to walk down Sea Face, passing by several people. Couples, children playing, people walking their dogs, elderly people out for walks. Vendors, selling corn, balloons and candy floss. The sky had now almost turned completely dark. The last of the sun's embers was fading over the sea. Rishabh and Saloni continued their conversation.

'And what else about IIT? Any girlfriends! Akash doesn't tell me anything,'

'Whoa! So many questions? Let me ask you some,' he said, escaping her questions. 'What was Calcutta like? Why Mumbai?'

'I went to an all girls school, then girls college and here too girls college for masters. So you're seeing a pattern here. Parents are strict but I'm totally daddy's girl. Bombay because I just needed a change. Besides, why should Akash have all the fun?'

'True! Any boyfriends?'

'Haha! The answer is hidden somewhere in the all-girl sanctuaries I just described, I guess!'

‘Hmm that sounds great, wish I could’ve joined,’ he said with a wink.

She slapped him playfully on the arm.

‘But actually there was this guy, Atul,’

‘Oh the plot thickens. How’d you meet him?’

‘You’re going to laugh but he was my brother’s IIT tutor,’

Rishabh turned to face her.

‘Tutor?’ he asked, raising a brow. ‘Am I sensing a trend here?’ he teased, nudging her shoulder with his.

‘I have no idea what you’re talking about,’ she said as they both smiled and looked straight ahead, continuing to walk.

The conversation continued until the light completely escaped the sky. As they started to head back home, their hands brushed together but neither of them said a thing.

As they approached her building, Rishabh said, ‘I guess that’s my cue, see you next week, same time?’

Saloni turned towards him and said, ‘That was fun, thanks, Mr Tutor,’ reaching out her hand for him to shake.

Rishabh impulsively kissed her.

When they pulled apart, she said, ‘Wow! That was unexpected!’

‘I guess the tutor line got me,’ he said, kissing her again.

‘Hi Akash!’ she screamed.

‘What? Where?!’ jumped Rishabh

‘Hahaha, *fattu*!’ she teased. ‘I better be seeing you before next week,’

‘Wait till next time!’ he said, tickling her.

He then got into a taxi and took a few seconds to process what happened.

I have a lot to tell Swan tonight, he thought excitedly.

❖

When Rishabh got home he was pleasantly surprised with the turn of events.

He pulled out his cellphone to see a message from Saloni. It was a meme of a guy leaning in to kiss a girl, but the girl lifts up her dog in front of her face thereby intercepting it.

He replied back. *She missed out! Good thing you didn't do the same.*

She sent the blush face emoji followed by a smiley.

He didn't respond.

Was that too much? Rishabh wondered. His hand holding the cellphone shook restlessly as he contemplated his next move.

Unable to conjure up something substantial, he did the next best thing which was, open the BOA app. Swan was waiting online.

His thumbs subconsciously tapped the button to initiate a game invite, before his brain could even catch up.

'There he is!' She squealed to herself.

'Hey!' He called out.

' Hi, so before we play I want to tell you something,' she said.

'Me too!'

'Well… I'll get right into it then,' she said, clearing her throat.

'I just thought, well you know, we've been talking for a while and I'm curious to see what you look like,' she said, ending the last few words quickly.

Rishabh was taken aback.

'Did I hear that correctly? *You* want to see a picture? Of *me*?'

'Don't make it so awkward, I'll show you my picture too.'

Rishabh raised his eyebrows and then let out a chuckle.

'I'm just surprised since you've been so secretive,'

She sighed. 'Do you want to do this or not? Speak promptly or forever hold your peace,'

'Hahaha! This is what I love about you. Let's do this!'

'Okay, so let's count to five out loud and then, change our profile pictures in the game so it updates at the same time. We can leave the picture on for ten seconds and then, take it down. Cool?'

'Sure let's do it!' Rishabh responded excitedly.

Her profile picture disappeared revealing an image of a young and beautiful girl. Her jet black tresses flowed down the shoulder pads of a motorcycle, black leather jacket. Her almond shaped eyes were neatly defined with winged eyeliner and her ruby lips were left natural without makeup. She didn't need it. She wasn't exactly smiling, but it wasn't a half smile either, maybe a quarter smile? Is that even a thing?

Before Rishabh could further analyse, the image was gone.

'Wait, what... it hasn't been ten seconds!' he said, slightly disappointed.

'Yeah but you cheated! That's not a picture of you, it's Ranbir Kapoor!'

Her image had him forget his silly prank. 'Oh, hahaha!' he laughed.

'So, are you going to upload the picture or not?'

'I'll do it if you also upload yours again.'

'Okay,' she said grumpily.

He proceeded to actually upload a picture this time. But she didn't.

'Hey! That's cheating!'

'No, it's not, just got you back for not uploading yours the first time,' she retorted giddily.

They got busy with the game and were cornered by an enemy squad in the wreckage area. The action was intense so the two stayed silent.

'It's my turn now!' Rishabh exclaimed suddenly.

'Actually I need your advice. I met a girl and we sort of kissed today,'

The firing stopped.

'Oh… what? Who?' she said, her voice perking up.

'Yeah, I know right? It was a bit impulsive, the way it played out. She's my best friend's sister and I was tutoring her and then we hung out after,'

'Oh, nice!' Sam's voice sounded like an odd mix of elation and boredom.

'We're texting right now and I'm not sure what to do next.'

'Well, why don't you take her out on a date?'

'Any ideas where?'

Silence resumed for a few minutes. The firing continued with increased intensity.

"Sam? You there?"

"Yeah sorry…"

'Well if I were in her place, I'd have liked to go to a comedy club. I think humour reduces the tension and awkwardness and makes the "getting to know each other" part a bit stress free.'

'Hmm, not a bad idea… Maybe I'll do that. Thanks Sam!' Rishabh said cheerfully.

Her avatar then sprinted towards the center of the action, guns blazing, but despite her bravery she was shot down and had to rescind a wounded soldier.

10
Virtually Yours

Rishabh and Bawarchi made their way to the Goenka residence at midday.

'How's it going, bro?' Akash enquired as they hugged and Rishabh placed Bawarchi on the table beside them.

'Alright, I guess. I'm really starting to worry about the progress of Bawarchi. There's still a lot of work to be done on the software side before I can even pitch it to an investor for the launch. And having a full-time job doesn't make it any easier. It's just all so screwed up, bro!'

'I'm sure it's hard, Rishabh. But I'm even more confident that if anyone can turn this into a successful venture, it's you. And don't worry about the investment part. As a matter of fact, I told dad about the robot a couple nights back and he is *so* excited to meet you and Bawarchi!' Akash's phone screen suddenly lighted up as he tried to quickly put it away.

'You already told your dad? Could have at least waited for me to implement the final touches!'

'I could have! But, dad sounded genuinely excited about your project. He asked when you were available for a meeting. Isn't that good news?' Akash waited expectantly for an answer.

'No, it's not!' The colour from Akash's face drained away.
'Oh sorry bro, I thought you would be excited.'

'It's *great* news!' Rishabh playfully bumped Akash's shoulder with his fist.

'Thank you so much, bro! That bit of news is seriously motivating. Although it does make me a little more anxious. I mean it's Mr Goenka. I have to impress him with my pitch.'

'*We* have to impress him with our pitch. Don't forget, we're partners bro. I'll talk to him and arrange a call for Monday.'

Akash tried to inconspicuously type something on his phone just in time for Rishabh to catch him in the act.

'Hey, get your head out of there man! What's going on? What are you trying to hide? Some new chick you're texting, or sexting?'

'Haha! It's nothing, no girl, no sexting. Just some work stuff I have to take care of. Why don't you eat something? I'll just be back in a bit,' Akash replied while still being deep in his phone. Rishabh could tell something was up for he knew the kind of hopeless liar that Akash was.

Hey Rish!! I did some reading last night and couldn't help but ask – are you made of copper and tellurium? Rishabh's phone lit up with a text from Saloni.

Umm..what? Rishabh responded.

Because I think you're CuTe! Geddit? Now that's a cheesy, nerdy one-liner I'd prefer over the boring hasee toh phase! ;-)

Rishabh couldn't help but smile. Saloni was flirting and how!

Phew! At least you're alive and well, I thought that one knocked you out cold. Rishabh replied.

Nah! I'm too hot.

Well, nobody can deny that! Total hottie! Rishabh thought out loud as he typed his reply.

'Who's the hottie?' Three distinct voices spoke in unison as Rishabh swirled around to find their owners.

'Gautam! Salman! What a surprise!!' Rishabh leaped across the room to embrace them in a bear hug. 'How did this come to be? I can't believe we're together here in person! It feels like ages since I last saw your faces!' Rishabh laughed.

'It was Akash who flew us here! He said your lives could transform with your robot launch! He begged us and paid for the flight, so we came!' Gautam declared.

'Never say no to complimentary airfare!' Salman concurred.

'And people say I can't keep secrets! See! This one here had no idea! I can do more than sext, baby!' Akash playfully nudged Rishabh in the ribs.

'Well, I knew something was up but I could have never predicted that you could use your brains to this effect. I'll take it back!' Rishabh patted Akash on the back.

'So, who was the hottie?' Gautam asked again. 'Don't think we forgot in the merriment!'

'You didn't tell me! Is it that BOA slayer – Brown Swan?' Akash exclaimed.

'Oh no, I was just checking out a model's handle on Instagram, bro! Chuck girls, let's talk about our venture.' Rishabh tactfully steered the conversation away.

'Bablu, get the beers out!' Akash ordered.

'Here's to old times!'

'And the present!'

'And our amazing future!'

'Cheers!' They all announced in unison.

❖

Back home, Rishabh hurriedly got his phone out to check for any messages from Saloni. Having come so close to getting caught red-handed by Akash, Rishabh had immediately put a pause to all the flirting and kept his phone securely locked, away from everyone's sight the entire time that he was at Akash's place with his boys.

The only message from Saloni was a wink emoticon. Rishabh had no clue how to turn this around to go back to their flirtatious banter that he enjoyed just a few hours ago.

'Why don't I ever know the good one-liners at the right time? Maybe I'll just ask Swan, she would definitely know some real good ones!' Rishabh enthusiastically turned on the game app and sent a message to Sam to come online. Only when she appeared online did Rishabh recall the awkward end to their last conversation.

'Hey,' Rishabh typed as he stretched out on his bed.

'Hey,' Sam replied.

'So, are we cool? You seemed a bit pissed the last time we spoke. Are things okay on your side of the world?' Rishabh asked, trying to sound nonchalant.

'Yeah, about that, I'm sorry I was just tired that night. Couldn't focus on the game, that's all,' Sam replied casually.

'Okay, if you say so. Thanks for your advice though. Comedy club really sounds great.'

'Oh, that advice! Yeah, sure, no worries!' Sam's avatar ruthlessly punched a soldier in the gut repeatedly.

'So, what's your favourite one-liner?'

'That's kind of random. What sort of one-liner?'

'You know, the flirty kind. I'm sure you must get hit on a lot. And all men use some. Which ones are most memorable according to you?' Rishabh asked very coyly.

'Okay, first, I hate one-liners. They're the cheesiest! Second, are you subtly asking me to help with your love life again? Because let me tell you, you aren't that subtle!'

'You got me! Guilty as charged!' Rishabh grinned and made his avatar wave at Swan.

'You're lucky I didn't shoot you right away. Anyway, sorry, no one-liners in my kitty. Why are you trying so hard anyway? Just be yourself. I'm sure if she's into you she'll not be expecting some cheesy one-liners but some real conversation and witty banter.' Sam abruptly stopped talking.

'That does sound like something any sane guy would do. You're right, I should drop the act and just be myself, you know, witty, as you put it.' Rishabh's wide grin was short-lived as Brown Swan punched his avatar in the gut with her gun.

'Hey! That was quite passive-aggressive,' Rishabh complained.

'Well, that's what you get for being too cocky. Can we just concentrate on the game for a while? I don't want to end up dead like last time. Or else I could add a player who actually knows how to play?' Sam chuckled.

Suddenly all Sam could hear was the panting breaths of their respective avatars and the sound of guns firing.

'Hey, did you die or did I just bruise your ego too blue?' Sam asked.

'Nope, just giving you what you asked for. My complete attention to the game,' Rishabh replied curtly.

In a matter of minutes Brown Swan and Kraken had taken over most of the island and Rishabh's swift moves had rendered over twenty opponents dead. Swan had never before noticed the ease and practiced moves with which Rishabh controlled his avatar.

With a final spinning kick and a headshot, Swan and Kraken won the game.

'Winner!' Rishabh exclaimed almost too excitedly.

'Wohoo! We did it Kraken!! I've got to say, you nailed this one! Too good, man!' Their characters high-fived on screen. Sam felt really elated by this win.

'You weren't half bad yourself. Although I could have handled the ten odd men that you killed all by myself. Just saying,'

In one swift motion, Brown Swan pulled the trigger, killing Kraken right that instant.

'Gotcha! Dinner is SERVED. If only you could have predicted that move! Guess handling ten odd men is easier than plotting this sinister a move, eh?'

'You did put my cockiness back in its place. But what a move! I've got to give it to you,' Rishabh replied simply as Sam felt him smile.

'That sounded quite mature of you. How rare! Makes me wonder if it's actually Rishabh I'm talking to or a robot suitably trained to talk respectfully to women?'

'Haha, it's very much me. Although I've also been trained to be respectful of women. Or haven't you noticed?'

'Talking about robots, I am building one, you know,' Rishabh suggested.

'My doubts have been confirmed. You really are a complete nerd. How weird a robot are we actually talking about? I'm curious,' Sam asked happily and relieved at once with the change of topic.

'I'll take that one gladly, nerd and proud! Don't know about weird, but it's definitely out of this world, or so I hope. He's called Bawarchi. Want to take a wild guess as to what he does?'

'Umm...bawarchi is a chef right? Wow! That does sound creative and peculiar!' Sam said, astonished. 'Are we really talking about a robot that can cook? You made it by yourself?' She asked completely intrigued.

'Well, some can cook. I can turn pieces of metal into culinary marvels! So, yes, I am the brains behind Bawarchi. Have I successfully impressed you?' Rishabh asked confidently.

'That is sort of impressive. How did you even come up with this innovation?'

'Let's just say food poisoning led me to my eureka moment. I hoped for an innovation that could eliminate poisoning risks in food and deliver the highest quality of food while abiding by the best levels of hygiene, so I set out to turn it into reality,'

Sam smiled to herself. 'I'm happy for you, dude. At least someone is closer to their dreams. You deserve to feel happy and confident after all the effort you must have put into your robot. And you got an investor! That's the hurdle most young entrepreneurs face.'

'Well, technically I don't *have* an investor yet. Just something in the pipeline. It could go either way. I have this pitch due for Monday.'

'I hear you. I'd recommend you prepare a failsafe. Like a safety net if your investor ditches you. Have you heard of Kickstarter? It's this online community that helps raise funds for creative projects by launching campaigns. It helps you quickly spread the word far and wide and money literally snowballs in. I'm sure there would be people genuinely interested and in need of a robot like Bawarchi,' Sam trailed off.

'Why did you stop?' Rishabh said smiling.

'Yeah, I know I just got carried away. But you should look into it.'

'I like how you sound when you're inspired. It's cute. And a *big* thank you for great advice yet again! I have heard of them but it never clicked. You're bright, Swan!'

There was that fluttery feeling again. Sam could feel her face warming up.

'As it turns out I do happen to have more urgent problems to tackle, for instance, finding another job.'

'You're looking for a job? You never said anything. Here I am blabbering away all my worries.'

'Yeah, it's because you never let me SPEAK!' Sam laughed.

'Hey! That's unfair! Who's the one always asking me to shut up and play and the one to disappear after every game?'

'Oh god! Such a drama queen you are. Yes, I am looking for a job. And now I really have to go tend to some personal affairs. So goodbye!' Sam said hastily and went offline.

What am I doing? Is it normal to get so close to someone through a video game? Sam pondered.

11
The Girlfriend

The honeymoon period of Rishabh's new relationship had begun. Stolen glances turned into stealthily clasped hands behind the back, tutoring sessions with a hint of footsie and a lot of dates snuck past under the guise of hanging out with Saloni's friend Trisha.

One evening seated at Burger Haven, Rishabh asked for Saloni's order.

'Aloo tikki burger obviously!'

'Can I ask you something?'

'Hmm…' she said, flipping through a Cosmopolitan magazine.

'Have you ever tasted chicken? Or rather, have you ever wanted to taste any type of meat? Just curious.'

Saloni furrowed her brows and scoffed.

'Of course I haven't. I don't want to go to hell.'

Rishabh chuckled. 'Okay, drama queen! But aren't you curious?'

'Yeah I guess I'm curious, but then I remember dad's face and the temptation is doused.'

'What? Saloni, you're not supposed to fear your parents. You're supposed to have a mutually respectful relationship,' he said, taking her hand.

'Weren't you supposed to get the burgers?' She said, withdrawing her hand and continuing to flip the pages.

Her gaze stayed down as she heard the creek of his chair when he ascended to place the order.

When he returned, he placed the tray on their table. As he pulled the chair back to sit down, a girl's voice boomed. 'Kraken Kulkarni!'

'Natasha?' Rishabh gasped as he spun around to hug the girl.

Saloni raised her eyelids ever so slightly to get a view of the girl. She was taller than Rishabh. She wore thick rimmed glasses with a military printed oversized jacket and a green hair band sat on her head like a crown.

Saloni continued looking down at her magazine but she couldn't resist looking up every two seconds.

'I'm working for the Ministry of Environmental Sciences now. We're headed to Indore next week where we'll be studying how we can regenerate some of our degraded forest land. Did you know that 45% of India's land is degraded?'

'Damn no! But thanks for the insight Miss Hippie,' Rishabh giggled.

Natasha lightly tapped his shoulder.

'I'm just kidding, you were always the smart one,' he said smiling.

Saloni started flipping through the magazine with greater speed and volume, but Rishabh and Natasha didn't flinch.

Frustrated, she grabbed a burger from the tray and started chomping down large bites at a time.

Natasha Gulati, his ex...

She recalled from the thorough social media stalking she had done.

'There weren't really any girls studying in mechanical engineering, so I had to venture out to life sciences, where I met Natasha,' he had told her.

As she continued to swipe through her Instagram feed, she had a moment of truth where she paused to check the wrapper of the burger she had just eaten.

Simultaneously, Rishabh spun around and said, 'By the way…'

Saloni ran frantically. She retched in the bathroom, almost driven to tears.

'Saloni, Saloni!' she heard a faint voice.

'Get out of the women's restroom!' an angry woman shouted.

'Sorry, aunty! Can I please stand here at the entrance with the door ajar please?' The women gave an angry stare and left.

'Saloni! Just listen, please!' Rishabh said, his voice fighting to be heard.

'What!? How could you feed me chicken, Rishabh? Is this some sort of sick prank?'

'Just come out and I'll explain, please Saloni!' he cried desperately.

'Why? Is Natasha still with you? Haven't you humiliated me enough?' Saloni continued ranting.

Suddenly there was silence.

Confused, Saloni opened the bathroom door to peer out. A group of women had formed a barricade around Rishabh, refusing to let him in.

'Ma'am, I swear I'm not a creep! I know someone in there!' he pleaded in vain.

Saloni giggled at his helplessness. As she exited the restroom, she signaled the women to let him go.

'Thanks for saving me', he said, dusting off his arms.

'You're not off the hook yet. Why'd you feed me chicken?'

'It's not chicken. It's Jain chicken! It's made of soy. I swear the Gujaratis here eat it as an alternative to meat. You said you wanted to taste chicken without sinning, and before I had a chance to explain, you'd eaten it. What happened anyway? You were eating it down like you hadn't seen food in months?'

'Oh!' said Saloni. 'And what about Natasha?'

Rishabh looked puzzled. 'What about her? I told her I had to go. I wanted to introduce her to my girlfriend but before I had the chance you were off running.'

Saloni's expression transformed from being angry to relieved in a second.

'Did you say, girlfriend?' She cocked her eyebrow playfully.

'Well yeah, I mean, that's what you are right? My girlfriend,' Rishabh rubbed the back of his neck sheepishly.

Saloni cracked a huge grin, forgetting the prior events in an instant.

'Now can we sit back down, please?' Rishabh said with a shy smile playing on his lips.

When they got back to the table, she inched her fingers forward to interlace with his and said, 'actually that Jain chicken was pretty delicious, thanks for doing that.'

'Of course it was, you diva,' he said, tightening his grip around her fingers.

'How did you even hear about this? Do you know any Gujaratis?'

'Yeah... Swan,' he said nonchalantly.

'Who?' she asked, confused.

'No I mean, I *saw* it on the internet,' Rishabh cleared his throat as he dodged a bullet.

'Oh! Okay.'

'Hey Rish, have you told my brother about us yet?' Saloni asked after a couple minutes.

'No, not yet, waiting for the right moment.'

'But when will that be? I don't want to lie to him for much longer.'

'Give me sometime. I know Akash, I just want to handle it sensitively.'

'Okay, I trust you,' she said and smiled considerately at him.

❖

Rishabh woke up with a jolt early Monday morning.

'That was the weirdest dream ever! I hope I didn't oversleep. Aah! Right on time!' He mumbled to himself.

He threw himself out of bed and bolted towards the bathroom with his phone in his hand.

'I need to go through my pitch a couple more times. Why can't I memorize stuff anymore? Stupid brain!' he exclaimed as he came across a message each from Sam and Saloni.

Sam: Hey dork, best of luck with your weird robot pitch today. It is this Monday, right?
Saloni: What do you call a snake that builds things? A BOA constructor! Haha get it?

Hmm strange! Rishabh could not believe that Sam remembered such an important detail of his life, especially when all they really did was play BOA. Saloni on the other hand seemed to not remember the same detail.

Anyway, more important things to focus on. Brain, wake up, will you? We can deal with the drama later.

Rishabh quickly texted a "thank you" to Sam and left Saloni on read as he spoke to himself in the bathroom mirror and practised his script. Ninety minutes later, Rishabh found himself in Akash's living room, perspiring like a hound, and muttering under his breath.

'Bro, will you chill? It's just my dad! I told you he is already sold on our idea. You need to cool down. We can do this together,' Akash said as he arrived with a cup of coffee in each hand and landed on the couch next to Rishabh.

Akash set up the laptop on the dining table as Rishabh gulped down some water and fidgeted with his collar and hair.

'Ready? We can do this, Rishabh. Just trust yourself,' Akash said as he connected the Skype call with Mr Goenka.

'Hi dad! How's it going? You look really good in that shirt I gifted you! Did you have a good breakfast?' Akash dragged on as Rishabh wiped his brow one last time and fidgeted with his shirt collar.

'Hi, *beta*. If you are done with the stalling should we get down to business? I have many more meetings to attend to after this. Is your friend here yet or not?'

'Of course, dad. Yes, Rishabh is very much here. He came much earlier to prepare. We're ready for you. Come on Rishabh, take it away bro!' Akash motioned for Rishabh to join him at the table and moved to the next chair.

'Good morning Mr Goenka. Thank you for meeting with us. I am so grateful that you could spare some time for us today. I'll try to keep this as succinct as possible. Thank you for this opportunity once again,' Rishabh declared with confidence.

Mr Goenka, despite his poker face, looked slightly impressed by the posed bravado at Rishabh's end. He signaled at Rishabh to begin his presentation with a motion of his hand and a barely-there nod. After delivering a very impactful pitch which was laden with a compelling motivation and a robust solution, he took a pause.

'I am ready for your questions Mr Goenka,' Rishabh said as he sat up a little more on his chair. He tried to subtly wipe off a patch of sweat off his forehead.

'Well, beta, first of all, you can relax now. This was a great presentation. Of course, I have some questions. Say, how big of an investment are you hoping for?'

Rishabh was taken aback by Mr Goenka's unexpected validation, but what surprised him even more was how straightforward this man was. Rishabh panicked. 'Umm sir...'

'Arre what sir, call me uncle, Rishabh. We are done with the formalities,'

'Sure. Uncle, I am actually looking forward to a significantly large investment ranging from fifty lakhs to one crore.' He clasped his hands fearing Mr Goenka's reaction. 'I will try to assemble and manufacture the robots in India itself, which will greatly bring down manufacturing costs, so this much seed money should cover it,' Rishabh said and fidgeted with his collar.

'Beta, I'd suggest you start thinking big. Don't limit yourself to the Indian market. I can see amazing potential here. You have no idea how many investors I can get interested in your robot. Think international – US, Europe, you are sitting on a golden egg. And believe me when I say this – you've not even scratched the surface! This is big money I'm talking about. Brilliant developers like you need an experienced hand on their shoulders, beta,'

'Sir... er, uncle, I don't know if I should think that far ahead yet...I mean there is still some work...'

'So, beta, work. Keep working on the completion. But the market won't wait. The biggest advantage you have right now is the novelty of your concept and the sheer absence of competitors. You need to start thinking further ahead and bigger. I say forget the fifty lakhs. That will get you nowhere. I would like to propose a five crore investment,'

What the f... Rishabh thought dumbfounded. He looked at Akash whose eyes were the size of golf balls now. *Was this really happening?*

'Five crore and we become partners – 75:25. Akash told me you two already had the partnership talk. So, why not make it official?' Mr Goenka eased back into his chair. There was a bemused look on his face as he scratched his beard with his free hand, the other cradling his phone.

Rishabh was still in a trance. He couldn't believe this conversation was really happening.

'Where are you lost, beta? Take the deal. I know what I'm talking about. I can get the paperwork started right away. Just remember, if you refuse this deal, that's it. Trust me, it doesn't get better than this. I have a ton of contacts in the US and European markets. You won't have to worry about a thing,' Goenka said without batting an eyelid.

Rishabh had to decide right away.

I wish dad was here. Well, what's the worst that could happen? It was Akash and his dad for god's sake! Who else could he entrust his project with if not them? More importantly, who would just offer five crores so quickly?

Rishabh looked over at Akash who nodded and grinned at him. *Of course, he could trust Akash! This was the dream team!*

'Sir, I'll take it. Thank you so much for your faith on us and on this project. I can't think of what more to say...'

'That's the way, boys. Good decision. Just quickly Rishabh, are there any patents or licenses that you're applying for?' Goenka asked as he appeared to collect his belongings.

'Yes, sir, sorry, uncle! I am yet to file the paperwork but I'll prioritize that now and let you know as soon as that's done.'

'No, beta, we shouldn't wait for that. I'll have someone call you for the details and set up another meeting in a few days for that. We should quickly start with the paperwork and get our contract sorted. That way you can get a portion of the funds immediately. I will need an email from you listing all details and specs of the robot. Send me the presentation as well. You should focus on completion more than anything else now. Got it?' Goenka said while simultaneously collecting his things hurriedly, looking in his phone and typing something on his computer. He looked up with his raised eyebrows now to take in Rishabh's reaction.

'Yes uncle, I understand that. I think you're right. Thank you so much for the advice already! I still cannot believe this is happening. Thank you!' Rishabh said with a genuine smile, his forehead now dry.

'My pleasure. Happy doing business with you, Rishabh and Akash beta. Now I have to run. Good luck and I'll get in touch soon.' Goenka waved a goodbye and immediately disconnected the skype call.

Rishabh took a deep breath and Akash erupted from his chair like a missile.

'Bro! We did it! We are going to be so rich! Dream Team!'

Rishabh couldn't help but give into Akash's enthusiasm. He jumped up from his chair and hugged Akash.

'This calls for a party bro! I'm calling the boys. Cancel everything! Let's drink to our future success!'

❖

Few hours later Akash, Gautam, Salman and Rishabh found themselves perched on the terrace of Kala Ghoda. A couple beers down, the boys took in the cool and humid air as they each took a swig of the doobie that they shared amongst themselves.

Rishabh was engrossed in his phone, staring at it blankly, checking it every couple minutes in the hope to hear back from Sam. It had been some time since he told her how well the meeting went. The other part of his brain was trying to figure out a way to make Saloni take a detour from nerdy one-liners and chicken jokes and talk about real stuff.

'Long gone are the days when hangovers couldn't get the best of me. I think I'm ageing at an accelerated rate. This is my last beer if I want to wake up without a headache. I have a flight to catch tomorrow,' Salman said as he chugged down the rest of his beer.

'Since when did you become such a lightweight, Sallu?' Rishabh mocked Salman with a grin and punched him on the arm.

'Yuck! Stop calling me that! Are you drunk already? Great to see your head finally out of your phone, by the way! Tell me again, who are you dating?' Salman punched Rishabh playfully in his gut.

'Hahaha! Not that drunk yet, bro! But I'm not dating anyone! #singleforever' Rishabh pretended to frown.

'C'mon. We've known each other long enough to know when any of us is lying! You can fool Akash but not us!' Gautam said groggily, rubbing his eyes with one hand, joint in the other.

'So? Who is she? Or is it a he? We're totes cool, bro!' Salman egged on Rishabh as they all seated themselves.

'*Chal*, you have to tell us now. Akash will be gone for a while based on how much he had to drink today. We're not ending this trip without you spilling the beans on what's got you so hooked to your phone.'

'And don't you dare say it's BOA. Because we know that can't be it!' Salman chided.

Rishabh rubbed the back of his neck, a forced smile on his face. 'Wow, you guys really know me, huh? I'll just say it's very much a "she". Thanks for all the support!'

'Well we had to ask. Can't be sure about anything these days!' Salman joked and Rishabh faked a laugh.

'Acha, let him talk na! Can you shut up for two minutes? Rishabh you were saying? Wait, I know who it is! It's that girl from BOA!! What was her name again?' Gautam gushed excitedly, a hand on his forehead and his eyes shut, forcing himself to think.

'Swan? No! God, you're screwed up! It's not her!'

'Oh well, who is it then?' Gautam persisted.

'Look, it's new and I don't exactly know what it is. So, I'll respect my girl's right to privacy!' Rishabh said softly yet sternly.

'Give us something na. Is she younger, older, hot, short, tall?' Gautam asked hastily.

'She's a little younger than us. Cute *and* hot,' Rishabh said with a smirk on his face.

'Well, any action yet?' Salman asked, nudging Rishabh with his shoulder.

'Not that it's any of your business! But honestly, no. I really don't know how!' Rishabh raised his hands and the beer in the air momentarily and put them back in his lap.

'Well there's always *Sex for Dummies*!' Salman interjected and they all laughed together. The four friends kept drinking, having fun and reminiscing their old memories.

Finally home late into the night, Rishabh silently made his way to his bedroom where he jumped straight on his bed, stretched like a starfish. Almost asleep, he was jolted awake by the constant vibration of his phone.

Lazily getting his phone out of his back pocket and in front of his face, Rishabh's eyes barely opened to the string of messages from Sam and Saloni.

He decided to quickly read Saloni's first, but his worsening hangover took the better of him and kicked him far away from consciousness.

❖

What the hell was that!

Rishabh woke up sweating profusely. His head hurt and he felt sore everywhere as if he had run a marathon. His volume was enough for his mother to know he was up.

'Beta, are you finally awake? Don't you have work today? It's 9.00 a.m. Should I get you anything?' His mother's voice grew louder and closer.

Rishabh frantically looked at the clock and put his dead phone to charge. He quickly sat back in bed and covered himself under his blanket just in time for his mother to knock and walk in with a cup of coffee.

'Morning, mom! You're a life saver! Thanks for the coffee!' Rishabh said and got up. Since, he was feeling sick, he decided to stay at home. After a quick shower, another mug full of coffee and a delicious homemade breakfast, he picked up his phone to call in sick to work. He couldn't wait to get started on this project.

Perched on his sofa, Rishabh now had time to finally go through the messages on his phone. After typing in a quick bon voyage to the boys, he finally sat reading Saloni's messages.

So, you have time to paint the town red with my brother, just not enough to reply to my messages? Guess you should date him instead!

'You seriously left me on read? Again???

'Rishabh, are you even alive? Or is the coroner reading these messages?

'Fine. Don't reply. I'm done,

'Uh oh. I am in trouble. Big time!' Rishabh couldn't help but laugh reading the messages. Saloni was really a drama queen!

Good morning, hottie! Has the steam finally stopped coming out your ears? I dreamt of you last night. Wanna know what it was? Or how it was?

Saloni appeared online as soon as the message was delivered. She appeared to type but suddenly went offline.

Aha! I'm being given a taste of my own medicine. Rishabh smiled to himself. If only I was a little more smooth!

Hey, I'm sorry. I was dead tired last night. And I woke up with the worst hangover of my life. I did read your message, but I could barely look at the phone. So typing anything at that godforsaken hour would have been a real feat! I'm sorry. How can I make it up to you?

Oh please don't bother, Rishabh!

He quickly dialed her number and walked to his bedroom. He was about to give up when Saloni finally picked up on the last ring.

'Hey you! How's my girl doing? I'm really sorry babe! I should have texted you. Or at least not left you on read! Lesson learned,' He paused to gauge Saloni's reaction.

Absolute silence.

'Hey, you there?' Rishabh moved his phone away from his ear to check if the call was still connected.

'Yup!'

'Saloni, *yaar*, I said that I'm sorry. I mean it. I want to make it up to you. Just tell me how! Look, you have to talk to me. We need to communicate. How would I know what's going on in your head. I'm sorry, Saloni, truly!'

To this, Saloni gave a very fake laugh.

'Hearing *you* talk about communication is quite funny. I'm sorry, I'm confused. Was it me who lagged behind on communication? I thought it was the other way round.'

'No, you're right. But is it any use getting stuck up on this? We should try to get over this and go out for a night to celebrate.'

'Whatever,' the monosyllabic replies were getting monotonous for Rishabh.

'So, I was at your place yesterday while you were at the gym. I finally had that meeting with your dad...about Bawarchi...you remember?'

'Stop stalling, will you? What happened?' He could feel Saloni's excitement through the phone.

'Nothing much. He just offered me five crores,' he said casually with a wide smile on his face.

'Oh my god! That's fantastic news, Rish! I knew dad would like you! It's happening! I'm so happy for you. We should definitely celebrate.' Saloni was clearly ecstatic. 'Although I should get more annoyed by your tardiness. Thanks for telling me a day later!'

'I know! I wish I could have told you earlier. But I saw your text when I was running late for the meeting. I was super nervous. And after the meeting I just didn't remember. Sorry!'

'It's okay. I'm sorry too. If only I knew something so awesome was happening for you! I am so happy that I want to see you now!'

'I've finally won over another member of the Goenka clan and how! I never knew I was so irresistible,' Rishabh said with a big smile.

'Oh you have no idea! So my brother was with you all through this?'

'Yeah, and later I just went out with the boys. Gautam and Salman were in town for just another night so it seemed like the perfect celebration.'

'So, you went out with your nerdy friends and couldn't drop me a text even later? I mean your girlfriend didn't cross your mind even once during this *perfect celebration*?'

'You did, multiple times. But you don't know how the boys are. I can never be sure of who has my phone at any given point. And to top it all, I was with Akash. He still doesn't know about us and I don't want him to think that I went behind his back. He's one of my closest friends and I want to tell him when the time is right.'

Saloni was silent for a while. 'You're right. I guess I was just jealous that I wasn't the first to know and celebrate with you because that celebration would have been way different. If you know what I mean!'

Saloni's voice grew huskier and Rishabh's breath escaped his mouth.

'Anyway, you shouldn't be scared of Akash. He can't lift when he's conscious so when he is around booze. But next time, if you don't text me... '

'I will be dead before I miss your text! Point noted.'

After the call, Saloni was on cloud nine. Rishabh would now spend even more time at her brother's place to work on the project. She couldn't help but ruminate about the time they could spend together alone. She had to ensure that her dad approved of him and with this successful beginning, things were on the right track.

I have got to start thinking of something to keep Akash out of the house as much as I can. A personal trainer could do just the trick, keep him out and busy for a good part of the day. Nights were tricky though.

I can't let Akash know. At least not for the next few months. Got to think hard and fast!

Saloni lay down in her bed painting pictures and conniving a fool proof plan.

❖

Rishabh had spent an enjoyable day at home. He was so immersed in the discussion with his parents that he forgot to check his phone. He looked at his phone and almost immediately thought of Sam.

'Shoot! I totally forgot to respond to Sam!' He spoke to himself while rapidly scrolling through the messages on his phone.

Yo! How did it go? Crying that you lost it or went so good that it got to your head?

The message from Sam instantly made Rishabh smile.

'Hey Swan! I was just thinking of you! Believe it or not, your wishes worked, and I got the deal!'

'Rishabh? Are we in BOA? My wishes didn't work. You see, I actually hoped for you to get trashed, like real bad! Just kidding!'

'Hahaha! Well in that case I say please keep wishing the same. Because if getting trashed translates to getting a million-dollar investment, then may the Universe keep trashing me!'

'A million-dollar what???' Sam was dumbfounded.

'Whoa, am I talking to the right Rishabh? How did this nerdy creep turn into a millionaire overnight? Did I wake up in a parallel universe?'

'Maybe we both did! And look who's all nerdy now – talking about parallel universes and what not!'

'Guess it's true what they say about company, been spending too much time with the king of nerds, have I not? Was supposed to happen sooner or later. Anyway, spill the beans!' Sam said excitedly.

'Ouch?' Rishabh sent over a puppy-eyed GIF to Sam that made her laugh too hard.

'Well, my investor, Mr Goenka, was blown away by our presentation. He could actually see the potential in this project that even I couldn't. He's prepared to aim high and brace for higher impact with his international clientele! So, he offered a five crore deal for the first leg of manufacturing and distribution. I still can't believe it's happening!'

A loud whistle escaped Sam's lips. 'Damn that's cool, dude! Congratulations! And not to sound like a damper to your dreams, but I hope you're staying vigilant! More power to you!'

'Yes, I was a bit nervous too. I mean, there was a point where I did second-guess the deal. But maybe I have to take a leap of faith for it to work, you know what I mean!' Rishabh said.

'I do. Just reach out if you require any reading between the lines. I have a lot of experience with financial contracts and would be happy to help.'

'That's really sweet of you, Swan! I might just take you up on it!'

'Sure. So, big celebration?'

'Done. Not going out like that anytime soon! I've had my fill of booze, food and marijuana for a whole year. Woke up today with the worst hangover of my life.'

'Wow. Your life's about to change, Kraken! Does it feel weird or awesome?'

'You're scaring me. It strangely feels like a bit of both. Which is why I want to start working hard on the project so I can stop feeling so much and concentrate on doing and delivering.'

'Hmm! I hope I too can experience that jittery feeling someday. Getting actual happiness and purpose from my work while also being super protective of it,' Sam said with a sigh.

'Hey, that reminds me. Last time we spoke you dropped this bomb on me – you're looking for a job? Why? Any luck so far?'

'Yeah, I'm currently an unemployed resident of the United States. I gave up my job in finance to focus on my lifelong passion of pursuing a career in music. Currently

I'm reevaluating my decisions and beating myself up while applying for any job that I can get that's even distantly related to music. I think my best option might be pursuing it through a data or finance based position at a music label and then working my way in.'

'Wow. You're really gutsy and brave, Sam.'

A calmness suddenly spread over her. 'That's polite of you,' she replied.

'I'm not just being polite. I seriously mean it. Personally, I don't know anyone who would give up on a lucrative finance career to pursue their dreams. It requires a lot of determination and self-belief. How are your parents taking it? If you don't mind me asking?'

'Well, my mom is still not taking my calls, neither replying to my messages. My dad is the only sane one right now. Although with my invisible progress so far, I wonder how long his support will continue.'

Tears started filling her eyes involuntarily as soon as she hit send. She couldn't understand what came over her. Maybe it was the sudden release of tension and emotions that she was holding on to for so long. She wiped the tears away to read Rishabh's reply.

'Hey, I'm sure he understands. You're not alone, Sam. I'm sure your mom will come around soon too! Just hold on and keep pestering her with calls and messages. I guess that's the way with moms.'

Sam had to put her phone away at this point. Her eyes were like wells overflowing with saline water.

'What is wrong with me?' she yelled out. This sudden release of emotions was so shocking that it made her giggle. She craved for some human touch – her mother's caress, a friend's hug, anything to soothe her. few ten minutes, when her sobs had softened, she picked up her phone and took a deep breath.

'Hello? Sam? Are you okay?'

'Are you crying? I'll let you be. Ping me, I'm right here,'

'HOW DID YOU KNOW?' She typed smiling and wiping away the last remnants of those stray tears from her face. Rishabh instantly appeared online.

'I didn't. I just guessed how that message must have felt. It's not easy to live alone and fight all your battles by yourself. Add to it the hardships and mental turmoil of leaving a job and frantically hoping and holding on to your dreams for a happier future. It turns you into a coconut. Hard on the outside, soft on the inside.'

'Sheesh, another one of your mushy theories, Rishabh.'

'Are you smiling now, Sam?'

'More like sympathizing with your sense of humour.'

'Hahaha, that works too. Look, I can't even imagine what it must be like for you. I really don't know much about the music industry either so I won't be pretentious and give you unsolicited advice. I'm sure you've had your fill by now. But I will say this – ask for help when you need it. Talk to your friends and family as much as you can. Don't confine yourself. Just try your best to keep your mind busy – good thoughts only. And come and kick some ass on BOA whenever you feel down and out.'

Sam's stomach felt like a network of knots.

'Thanks for the pep talk! *Baaki* ka I can't promise, but I can definitely kick your ass on BOA anytime. I have to get down to following your plan to an amazing and positive life now. Starting with calling my mom and facing some daily rejections.'

'Cool, I'll leave you to it. And you'll experience that feeling soon – the weird yet awesome one. Trust me. <3'

Sam dropped her phone on her bed.

It does not mean anything. It's just friendly, platonic love. Not even love, just an emoticon.

12

Saloni? Who Knew?

Saloni and Rishabh had been dating for a month. She was ready to take their relationship to the next level. Rishabh was everything she wanted in a boyfriend. Smart and sensitive. The added bonus was that he was now dad-approved, well, to some extent.

They revelled in the excitement of keeping their relationship hidden from Akash. The late-night sneaking, the mid-business interruptions, and the playful flirting – sometimes even in Akash's presence – gave Saloni a strange kick. She was well aware of the dangerous grounds that she was treading with Rishabh, but this peril felt amazingly sexy.

Saloni was ready to go the whole mile with Rishabh. She was nervous, yet excited, and wanted it to be a night to remember.

'Let him take the lead,' her friend had suggested. But Saloni had other plans. She wanted this to go her way, just like everything else did. She sat down at the dining table and pulled up her Pinterest board.

Okay, what does he like? Lingerie, candles, whips? Hmm... no! I don't want it to be cliché.

Then it struck her.

He does like to play BOA! Maybe watching me play it could be a turn-on? Something he would never imagine me to do.

She downloaded the BOA app on her iPhone immediately. She had never been much of a gamer but she was eager to impress her man. She started the game and was immediately overwhelmed.

OK... what else can I do? she thought as she tapped her chin.

'Wait a minute!' She exclaimed as she had another eureka moment. She could dress up as a kinky version of Rishabh's favourite BOA character that night!

Once her mind was made up, she put her plan into action.

First she rang Rishabh to invite him to her place tonight which he readily agreed. Then, she excitedly embarked on a shopping spree with a list in hand.

By evening, she was ready for a night of passion and intimacy. She looked like Xena, the warrior princess. She wore a red bra with a black leather cropped vest revealing her toned stomach. She had a metallic belt wrapped around her rib cage holding *shuriken* (ninja daggers). The outfit was completed with knee length, lace up combat boots and fingerless gloves clutching a fake submachine gun. She looked in the mirror and acted out some ninja stances – upping the sex quotient in her mind.

By 8.00 p.m., she completed the last touch to her outfit – a giant metal helmet, covering her eyes and revealing only the lower portion of her face, smeared with bright red lipstick.

She saw Rishabh arrive in the doorway. To set the mood, she played some video game themed music apt for the night.

He couldn't see her because she was hiding in the nook of her mirror across from the closet.

'Hold fire, captain!' she said loudly, trying to sound as sexy as possible.

When she finally revealed herself she saw a look of surprise on his face.

They quickly inched forward to kiss and BAM! Her helmet collided with his head.

She used her quick reflexes to toss the helmet while he hurriedly pulled off his shirt and returned to grab her. His arms reached for her shoulders, but in a split second he was flying. He yelped loudly. Saloni looked down at the shurikens around her rib cage that had stabbed him.

This coincided with a voice from the speakers screaming "Finish him!" a line from the *Mortal Kombat* theme song.

Rishabh was now on the floor. Saloni turned her back to him. She began to cry when she felt a familiar, calming touch on her shoulder.

'I'm so sorry babe...' before Saloni could phrase her apology, Rishabh took one look at her face and dropped on the floor again. She winced as she saw Rishabh giggling uncontrollably on the floor, shaking profusely, like a wet dog. She cautiously took off the metallic belt that housed the ninja stars and threw it under the table.

'Did you get a concussion from the helmet? What's so funny?'

'You! Oh god, look at your face! It's like you've seen a ghost,' Rishabh tried to sit up, his vest around his belly stained with blood as he repressed his laughter. He spotted the remote to the speakers nearby and turned off the theme track.

'I thought I killed you! How badly are you hurt? Wait, let me see,' Saloni carefully rolled up his vest to take a look at the damages. An audible sob left her lips and Rishabh hugged her tight.

They looked at each other and kissed passionately. Rishabh's hands mussed Saloni's hair and slowly found their way to the black leather vest that he started unbuckling. A sigh escaped Saloni's mouth and she bit Rishabh's bottom lip quickening his movement on the leather vest buckles. She reached to push his vest over his head.

With the vests off, they went back to kissing. Rishabh lay down on the floor as Saloni climbed on top of him and ran her hands over his chest and shoulders. He sighed and got up instinctively, trying to get all clothes out of the way. The sudden motion hit his belly hard and out came a scream that scared Saloni off of him.

'Where did I get you now?'

'It wasn't you, I got up too fast. Ouch!' He winced in pain.

'This is now how I pictured this. Why can't I do anything right? I really wanted to impress you. But not like this.' Saloni put her head between her knees and wrapped her hair in a bun. She was getting a headache from this ridiculous night.

'Maybe tonight is not the night, babe. We'll have many more. Our first will be special. Although I'm not sure it will be as memorable as tonight.' He tried his best to not laugh.

'Did you like any of it? I should have tried harder to learn how to play BOA than assaulting you as a character from it! I'm the worst girlfriend!'

'I liked most of it. Except the stabbing part, for obvious reasons', Rishabh joked as Saloni sat unamused. 'Look, these things happen, I'm sure. First times are always tricky, I guess. And you tried to play BOA? Why?' He looked at her amused and confused.

'Because I know how much you like it. I wanted to be a part of it. I guess I wanted you to like me more?'

'I really like you Saloni. Why can't you see? And I don't expect you to like or get everything I like. That's unfair. BOA can stay away when we're together.'

'I just didn't want to lose out to it.'

'Lose out to a video game? You're my girlfriend! There *is* no comparison!'

Saloni smiled coyly and Rishabh kissed her again.

❖

Later that night, after reaching home Rishabh got into his bed and examined his wounds thoroughly. The way the evening had unfolded had made his mood grumpy.

Why did Saloni have to have those ninja stars fastened to her body? Oooh! That body though! He fantasized about her toned belly and legs for a moment.

But no, isn't it strange and just plain desperate of her to be jealous of a stupid game? Maybe I am just missing out on some other detail. He thought.

'She is young and gullible and I need to be a bit more patient and understanding, I guess. But how do I turn this around? Our first time needs to be special!' He muttered to himself. As he was lost in thoughts, he didn't realize when he slept. He woke up only when his phone buzzed where he saw the BOA invitation from Sam waiting for him. He promptly plopped on the bed and accepted the invite.

'Hey Swan! Isn't it daytime there? No work today?'

'Well, Kraken, what can I tell you? I have absolutely nothing to do! Wanna play or not? Focus on the game! Duck!' She yelled right before Rishabh's head exploded from a bullet in the game.

'Never seen anyone bomb this game so badly in the first thirty seconds! Well done! Where's your head at, nerd?'

'Sorry, I really don't know what's come over me or actually I do,' Rishabh added hesitantly, his free hand brushing his neck.

'What is it?'

Rishabh asked if she was sure she had nothing better to do before he told her his sad little tale of how he got severely injured whilst trying to make love to his girlfriend.

Sam laughed loudly at the story which left Rishabh embarrassed.

'What can I do? Help me, Sam!'

'Maybe she did all that to impress you. It's alright. Weird that it turned you on, but I'm not judging!'

'It's Saloni's first time and I know she wants it to be special so I want to make sure she feels comfortable and stuff.'

'Did you guys not talk about this?' she asked worried.

'Umm...no, why would we!'

Can't believe people these days, she thought to herself. She tried to adopt a gentler tone with him so as to not scare him away.

'See it doesn't have to be this difficult. You know her personality, right? What does she like?'

'I know she likes Ariana Grande's songs and fashion, burgers, makeup, working out... ' Rishabh replied thoughtfully.

'Wait! That's not her personality. That's just what she likes!'

'I honestly never really thought about it, and yes, I'm aware how shallow that sounds. We've been together for a month now and all we do is make out and flirt.'

'Wow, you don't need a girlfriend for that you know, Rishabh!'

That rendered him speechless. Sam had identified the root cause of the problem. Is this the real reason he felt so awkward and why they couldn't do it tonight? Sam analyzed the silence and Rishabh's discomfort.

'Maybe, you need an evening to get to know her better – that's where intimacy comes from,' she suggested to Rishabh. She would have to spell it out for him.

'But what do I do?' He asked and instantly regretted how stupid that sounded.

'Look, I don't know her personally, so… '

'Okay, what would you like?'

'If that helps, I would like to meet for a drink and some appetizers, attend a stand-up show, take a stroll along the beach, or Marine Drive in your case, go back home and chill!'

'Woah! That does sound nice!' Rishabh said excitedly.

'It's nothing out of the blue, really, very basic, I know! But sometimes, especially in your case I think, it helps. You don't need to plan something phenomenal! All you need is some downtime, comfort and intimacy. Trust me, think simple and intimate.'

Sam stopped speaking as she was prodded out of her daydream, hoping she sounded as coherent as possible. That fluttery feeling in the pit of her stomach was coming back. She gulped down some water and looked out of her window to distract herself.

'I think you're bang on. You're the best, Sam! If you were here, I'd take you on that date just to thank you!'

'Haha no worries, nerd!' She tried to sound as nonchalant as possible.

'What are your plans for the day?'

'Well, I'm kind of fiddling with the idea of driving down to Irvine – that's where my parents stay.'

'That sounds like a superb plan, Sam. Did your mother take your calls, if you don't mind me asking?'

'Well, yesterday when I called her, my dad answered after he found it ringing in the living room. He suggested that I better make a face-to-face apology that she just cannot ignore or run away from.'

'Your dad keeps sounding better and better!' Rishabh exclaimed laughing.

'Haha, yeah, I think in the midst of this delirium, he definitely is the only one retaining his wisdom.'

'Then I think you should listen to him. Well, good luck with your mom!'

'Good luck with your girlfriend! She laughed hard.

❖

After the call with Rishabh, Sam decided to catch up with Neha and her string of messages.

'Hey Sam, where have you been? You didn't even react to those hilarious gifs that I sent you three days back!'

'Sorry, Neha! It must have slipped my mind! There's a lot going on, you know, especially since I started taking these online classes for advanced drum players. Plus being unemployed really screws up your sleep cycle. I can never keep a tab on my own schedule as a result.'

'Are you okay? Any progress? I know it's too soon to ask, but still,' Neha asked gingerly.

'Nothing yet, I do have a couple interviews lined up for next week though, so let's see! Listen, I'm coming home. You have to be there! I need to see you and talk to you about something urgent. I'll deal with the mess at home, but there's something else,' Sam said almost coyly.

'Oh boy, don't tell me. Is it about that nerdy gamer boy? Oh Sam, you're a lost cause!' Neha giggled.

A couple hours later, Sam was ready to drive away. She got in her jeep and took a deep breath.

We have to do this, Sam. I need to win over my mom.

With the freeway almost free of traffic Sam made it to her parent's place in Irvine.

Her dad was quietly sitting with a book on the armchair when she unlocked and entered the door.

'No Diwali lights this time around?' She quipped, hugging her old man.

'No, we decided to keep them tucked away safely, lest they may attract some more Gujarati bachelors,'

'Like a moth to a flame!'

Her dad brought some cold coffee and homemade snacks as Sam searched for her mom around the living room. 'Don't tell me I came all this way only to find her at some aunty's place?'

'Your mom is very much at home, but she's a step ahead. She caught you getting out of your car while she was leisurely looking out of the window. She instantly got up and strode to the bedroom. I knew it was your car in the driveway.'

'So, you didn't tell mom that I was coming?'

'Did you want her to run away altogether? Anyway, how have you been? Prepped up for those interviews?'

Sam just couldn't do it this way. She needed both her parents here. 'We're going in!' she got up briskly from the sofa and headed towards the room.

'Hi mom! Guess who's here? Your favourite *bacha*!' She tightly hugged her mom whose eyes were now the size of golf balls. She was struggling to get out of her tight hold.

'Stop it! Leave me, Samira,' Alka exclaimed so sternly that Sam let go instantly.

'Stop pushing me away, mom. What *is* my mistake? Wanting something better in my life? Or having the courage to pursue my dreams? Shouldn't you be supporting me? I need you, mom. Can't you see I can't do this alone?'

'Of course, you can. You don't need me! In fact, you don't need anyone! You don't even want to get married! You can make all your decisions and just come here and declare what you've chosen to do,' Alka said with her eyes fixed on the wall, her voice breaking.

'Well, you're wrong! I need my support system, and that includes you guys. I can do *anything* if I have you guys backing me,' she said putting a hand over her mom's shoulder.

In a moment of pure and unbridled emotion, Alka swept Sam into her arms as tears started streaming down both their faces.

'I am so scared for you, Samira. You had such a well-paying job. What will you do if it fails?' She said between sobs, still holding Samira tight in her arms.

'I'm scared too, mom. But I cannot afford to think about the failing part yet. We all need to focus our energy on getting this right. It won't be easy, I know! But with you two, I can do anything!'

'In fact, Samira has already started for jobs and even has two interviews scheduled for next week. They are really big companies too. Which ones were they again?'

'One's at Akedo Media and the other at Quincy Jones. Wait, I'll show you!' Sam took her phone out of her pocket to show her parents the company websites as her mom loosened her hold on her, but not letting go completely.

'I'm sorry I wasn't more supportive,' Alka added a moment later and Sam gave her a warm hug.

❖

'How did it go at the Patel residence? I hope you did not annoy Alka aunty and Rajesh uncle anymore?' Neha asked as Sam greeted her with a long bear hug.

'Well you'll be surprised to hear this but I handled it pretty well! I had a script prepared. I knew what I wanted to say and tried my best to control my emotions. I was able to win them over. It feels as if a huge rock has been lifted off my chest. I realized I had to win her trust by admitting how truly terrified I am.'

'And how did you come to this awakening?' Neha asked suspiciously.

'Honestly, by talking to Rishabh.' Neha went silent.

Sam disclosed how he had been there for her through the last one month of her life.

'I can't help but feel a connection with him. I don't want to overcomplicate this in any way, trust me. But when I talk to him, I feel heard and understood which has never happened with a guy before. He gets me and always says the right things. Well, most of the times, if you don't count his dumb puns and nerdy jokes,' she said and laughed to herself, recalling one of his nerdy jokes.

'I think what's nice about meeting people through a video game is that there's no pressure that comes with online dating. When people go on apps with the intention of finding love, there are superficial expectations which actually force people to conceal their true selves. But when you're gaming, you just go with the intention to play so the conversations are breezy and genuine.'

'That makes sense *but* at the risk of repeating myself, you're a lost cause Sam!' Neha declared.

'Look at you! I have never seen you more relaxed and happier. You have been smiling ever since you got out of your car. I also think that maybe, he is the right guy for you. What do you think?'

'I don't know about any of that, but I do know he definitely *isn't* with the right girl!'

'What? He has a girlfriend?' Neha asked, genuinely shocked.

'Yeah, although they haven't sealed the deal yet, if you know what I mean – I was just suggesting intimate date ideas to him just last night.'

'Hold it. *You* were suggesting date ideas to a guy you have feelings for?'

'Neha, are you listening to me? I don't have "feelings" for him!'

'Yeah, that's exactly what we've discovered in the last ten minutes. Sam, I'm truly concerned. What are you doing? Also, what did you suggest they do?'

Sam told her everything.

'So basically, he takes this girl out on *your* dream date? You have a big heart, my friend, but the tiniest brain! Stop spurring his love life! You need to tell him.'

'I will do no such thing. We're just friends. I have other matters to focus my time and energy on.' They both fell quiet for a minute as a plane flew over and they looked up at the open blue sky.

Sam broke the silence. 'At twenty-six, I cannot waste more time on matters of the heart while I sit unemployed.'

❖

Rishabh's idea of a night of passion had worked perfectly for both of them so far. He had texted her late last night leaving only necessary information at her disposal – the location she had to meet him for drinks – Mockingbird on Marine Drive sharp at 7p.m.

He had booked a booth and arranged for her favourite songs to play all through that first hour. He also ordered her favourite food and later took her for a stroll along Marine Drive. There, he started singing and twirling her around.

'No Rish! I don't dance in public. People will stare and think we're hooligans.'

'No, they'll think we're young and in love.'

The weather had played accomplice to his simple romantic date plans. Now, all he had to do was make sure that Akash was out of the house before they headed back there together. It had been challenging, yet fun, so far to pretend to teach Saloni on Tuesdays and sneak kisses and amorous looks in his presence.

Today, Akash was strategically sent off on a date that, unbeknownst to him, had been set up by Rishabh. Kiara from college had a huge crush on Akash all through college and happened to be in Mumbai for the week. It had worked so brilliantly!

Knowing Akash, Rishabh was sure that he wouldn't be back until the wee hours of the morning or later. All he had to do was sneak out and with Saloni's help, that should be a cakewalk while Akash snored away.

Walking to Saloni's apartment was turning a little awkward for them both, or so Rishabh thought. They both knew what they were walking towards and that made him nervous with each step he took. He suddenly remembered what Sam had told him but he was unsure of whether this was the right time to bring it up. He went with his gut.

'So, are you tired or tipsy at all?'

'No, I'm okay. Are you alright? You're sweating so profusely. Is it too hot for you, I thought the weather was pleasant tonight?'

'I'm just nervous I guess,'

'What are you nervous about? It's just us and sex. This would have already happened ages ago if only our plans hadn't gone to the gutter!'

Boy, was she confident!

If there was one thing that Rishabh admired the most about Saloni, it was her confidence. It reflected in everything that she did, even the way she walked right now.

'So, what's the one thing you like about me the most?' He asked, trying to sound casual.

'Well, we're about to find out shortly!' she winked.

'Hahaha! No, I mean a personality trait. For example, I love your confidence. I think that's your greatest trait,'

'Hmm...thanks for that! Honestly, I really like your hair and your height. And your dimples too!'

'Okay, but that's about my looks, not my personality.' He looked at Saloni and she appeared nonplussed.

'I don't know, I never thought about it. Maybe I'll love how passionate a lover you are!' She gave him a quick peck.

'Hopefully,' Rishabh started deliberating over this. *Is physical attraction enough? How could Saloni not name a single thing about me?*

Finally at home, Saloni walked in first to check if the field was clear. She then waved at Rishabh to come in and headed straight for the kitchen after locking the door behind him.

She got a bottle of wine out along with two glasses at the kitchen counter.

'To our first time together and this night that's about to get even more lit!' She toasted and clinked her wine glass against his. They took a few swigs after which she led him to her bedroom, leaving the bottle and glasses on the kitchen counter.

Rishabh, although even more skittish now, got out a pen drive from his jeans pocket which had Saloni's favourite songs. He had a sensual playlist ready and plugged into Saloni's bedroom console to set the mood, beginning with Ariana Grande's *Into You*. That instantly turned Saloni on and she kissed him lightly on the lips.

They slowly started undressing each other when Saloni remembered Rishabh's comment about her confidence. She pushed him on the bed gently and gave him a surprise striptease. As soon as the song ended and another began, Rishabh pulled her towards him.

'I have never done this before.'

Saloni paused and looked him in the eye. He looked earnestly nervous, his mouth went dry. She took his hands and glided them all over her body.

'Well, in that case, let me show you how,' she whispered seductively close to his ear. Carefully unbuttoning his shirt, Saloni swayed her hips on his lap. She could feel him getting hard already. Finally undressed, with Saloni on top of him, they kissed and she tugged at his ear. He undid her bra, caressed and gently kissed her all over her neck and breasts.

'Tell me if this is okay. I'm not hurting you, right?' He suddenly stopped and asked.

'Stop thinking, just feel it.' Saloni brushed Rishabh's lips with hers as she pulled the covers over them. Thirty minutes later, they lay spent and smiling in each other's arms. Rishabh was running his fingers against Saloni's bare skin under the covers and she was taking in his scent.

'I love your perfume. Which brand is it?' she asked.

'Umm, I can't remember anything right now.' He smiled against her hair as she giggled and gave him a peck on the cheek.

'Was it good for you?' He asked nervously.

'As good as it will ever be.' They both fell asleep as the sky turned even darker outside.

❖

It was a little after midnight when Saloni woke up parched and went to the kitchen to get a bottle of water back to the room. As soon as she sat up in her bed, she heard some keys jangling and uneven heavy footsteps approaching. Petrified, she shook Rishabh out of his sleep.

'Rish, wake up!! There's someone out in the hall! Go and check. Protect me, wake up!'

Drained and groggy, Rishabh woke up hesitantly. Without much thought, he walked out yawning and rubbing his eyes wearing just his boxers.

'Rishabh? What are you doing here?' Akash was loudly slurring. He was visibly drunk and trying hard to focus on

Rishabh's silhouette in the darkness. His eyes instantly shot to the wine bottle on the kitchen counter and his brain immediately calculated what must have happened. Saloni walked out behind Rishabh, eager to get that bottle of water when she froze in her tracks on seeing Akash.

'Did you sleep with my sister?' Akash garbled incoherently pointing at Rishabh.

Words evaded Rishabh. The sleep deprivation and the shock of bumping into Akash in the middle of the night after having slept with his sister rendered him dumbfounded. Saloni discreetly formed a barrier between the two and tried to calm Akash down.

'Hey, Akash, are you okay? Come take a seat.' She helped him sit on the bar stool by the kitchen counter and got a bottle of water out of the refrigerator. Akash was staring at her coldly the entire time.

'It's not what this looks like, let me explain...'

'You, shut up. You speak!' He pointed towards Rishabh again. 'Did you sleep with my baby sister?' Akash swayed a little and was just about to crash on the floor when Rishabh leapt to protect his head from bashing against the counter first. Rishabh and Saloni dragged Akash to his room and quietly tiptoed back to Saloni's room.

Without wasting any more time or words, Rishabh quickly started dressing up and fervently hoped for Akash to forget what he witnessed tonight.

❖

Sam's trip home had been the best one yet. She had enjoyed a lavish, yet homely dinner with her parents and Neha, whom she invited over after their hour long catch up. She had spent the entire day without thinking about Rishabh, well after the talk with Neha. But this morning she felt a strange urgency to text or call him.

Hey Rishabh, my visit to my parents' home was amazing. My mom didn't disown me. Yay! I wanted to thank you, for boosting my confidence!

Rishabh's phone lit up. Having chosen to ride the last local of the night to his place, he was taking in the cool, humid air. He couldn't help but text back right then.

Hey, glad to be of help and to hear the good news! It went amazing at my end of the world too. If you know what I mean! Thanks for the date idea! He sent her a GIF of a heart exploding.

Sam quickly rushed to her beeping phone to look at the message from Rishabh. At once she felt vexed and threw her phone on her bed.

Neha's words came ringing back.

You were suggesting first date ideas to a guy you have feelings for?

13
The Revelation

Next morning, the sun rays woke Rishabh up at 9 a.m. He has never been more tired, but he also hadn't woken up happier.

He got out of bed to stretch his lean body and started playing *Here's Comes the Sun* on a music app on his phone. Beaming just like the bright day outside, he was replaying every single move he made with Saloni last night in his head.

Looking at his phone now, he came across Sam's name and expected to see a message from her, but nothing.

Just then he received a text from Saloni.

You need to talk to your best friend. He had the audacity to lock me in my room. I had to literally call dad to get his ego in check. Dad didn't say anything to me but you are dead. His words, not mine!

He read Saloni's message again. Of course, he knew this day would come.

The best thing would be to stay out of Akash's face a little longer. I could go over tomorrow and talk it out. He thought to himself while rubbing his neck. It had gone too sore after last night.

Saloni kept messaging him repeatedly.

Babe, I'm soooo scared, come here Rish please! I will only feel safe in your arms, He quickly typed a reply.

Babe, just calm down please. Have some water and watch a movie. He won't do anything. He's your brother, no matter how mad he is right now, but he obviously won't harm you! He's just a bit overprotective. Let him blow off some steam today. I'll be there tomorrow. Will get a six pack of his favourite beer and he'll be back to normal. Just hide anything sharp or hard when I'm there. He does have an insane temper!

Of late, Rishabh had been taking too many days off from work to finish the prototype of Bawarchi. There was just a couple days' work more to put in to develop the prototype until he could finally sit back and relax. Today seemed like a good day to stay home and work. Having texted his manager, Rishabh was neck deep planning for the day ahead when his dad knocked on his door.

He arrived with a tray, on it – tea, biscuits, namkeen, fruits. With shaking hands, he set the tray on the table and smiled at his simple accomplishment.

They sipped from their cups in silence for a couple minutes.

'So, are your work colleagues missing you at all or are you just working from home?' His dad asked, feeling his eyes on him and taking another sip.

'Working from home, yes. But not for them, for myself. I really cannot break my focus right now. I feel like I need to absolutely put in all my time and energy into this for the next several months. Once the prototype is complete, which should be soon, I will need to get into the manufacturing and business side of things.'

'Don't forget the legalities, the paperwork and contractual side of things, Rishabh!'

Yes, if I have to choose, I choose this over a job that I can get back after a couple years,' Rishabh said excitedly pointing at the paraphernalia of paper, circuits, and gadgets spread out on his bed.

'Well, if you have decided then it's time you act on it or are you waiting to get fired?'

'Yeah, I guess I was just waiting to talk it over with you.'

'Oh, so for resigning from a 9 to 5 job you have to ask me? But signing over your entire company to Goenka did not even require any second thoughts? Did I not warn you against signing over 25% of your company to your friend, Akash? But you went ahead and gave him and his dad a majority stake!'

'Dad, for the millionth time, I did not sign over my company to Mr Goenka! It is just seed money. Can't you see once this takes off, a five crore sum would be nothing but a fractional investment?'

'Where is the contract that says this?'

'Good you reminded me, another task to add to my to-do list of the day.'

Rishabh put a hand on his dad's shoulder and said, 'Dad, I know you're feeling overtly protective of me. And I love you for it. But trust me, I won't do anything stupid or reckless with this project.'

'Well, let's hope so!' Rishabh smiled lovingly at his dad.

Rishabh got back to work as soon as dad went away. The only constant distraction throughout the day was Saloni and her texts, more like sexts.

At around 3, he finally took a break from work and responded to her messages. A couple minutes passed when he asked her, 'So, were you a shy kid?'

'What? Why are we talking about kids?'

'Not about kids. Just you as a kid. I just think we hardly talk about ourselves. Intimacy stems from actually knowing the other person, or so I read somewhere.' He explained sounding awkward yet inclined.

'Oh, please don't start again! I really can't think clearly. You leave me so tired and sweaty, you know.' Rishabh went silent.

'Maybe we can talk tomorrow, at length, when you come over to win over your furious BFF?'

❖

Late in the evening, Rishabh hesitantly picked up the phone to call Mr Goenka to ask about the contract.

Mr Goenka picked up on the second attempt. Rishabh greeted him and tried to sound very casual while informing him that the prototype was close to ready. He was just calling to ask if the contract was going to be ready anytime soon.

'Arre beta, why are you so serious and stressed every time? Just chill beta. Everything good will happen at the right time. Just leave it to me. You focus on the robot. Do you need any funds transferred?'

'No sir…uncle, everything is okay…'

'I do want to see it working completely in person and so I am planning to come down to Mumbai. Will also get to meet Saloni and Akash after a long time. We will all go out and celebrate!'

'Yes uncle, sure!'

'Be more excited, beta. Your life is about to change. Keep me posted on the progress.' After saying that, Mr Goenka left the call.

Rishabh did try to make his dad feel like it's no big deal, but deep down, Rishabh was feeling a little iffy about Mr Goenka's whole stance on the contract.

'No Rishabh, you're thinking too much! Need to take a break, it's just in his nature. You shouldn't judge his sense of business or authenticity from the way he talks to you on the phone!' he told himself.

Later that night, he sat and typed out his resignation. He looked forward to Sam's text, but was too exhausted to stay awake any longer.

Need a good night's sleep to confront Akash tomorrow!

❖

On the way over to Akash's place, Rishabh couldn't help but keep going back in his head to the exact moment when he pressed send on his laptop and sent his resignation over to his manager. It had taken much more resolve than he had anticipated. He felt a mixed bag of emotions – relieved yet confused and scared.

At 1 p.m. he reached his destination. He took a deep breath before ringing the bell.

Saloni opened the door as soon as he knocked and hugged him tightly. She was evidently happy to see him. Even before Rishabh was able to completely walk in the door, she hungrily kissed his lips and looked up at him with a wide smile.

'Whoa isn't Akash around? Let's sort this out first!'

Akash cleared his throat. Saloni jumped up in fear and stood beside Rishabh. The tension in the room was palpable and Akash's cold stare made Rishabh let go of Saloni's hand. She folded her arms and looked at Akash.

'So, did you find your lost loyalty in my sister's mouth yet? Or do you need more time?' Akash asked sourly. Rishabh was dumstruck.

'Bro, I'm sorry. This is not how I wanted you to find out. I mean, ultimately. I wasn't going to go behind your back and...'

'*Go behind my back*? What else have you been doing then?' Akash bolted halfway across the room as his voice grew louder. Saloni moved from Rishabh's side to his front to stop Akash from coming any closer.

'Step back, Akash,' Saloni tried to pacify him.

'Oh please, I don't talk to hoes.'

'Akash, it's your sister,' Rishabh said, clearly appalled.

'You don't teach me. I know Saloni well enough to accuse her. Regardless of what happened, there's some unspoken boundaries we set in our friendship. She's off limits bro.'

'How dare you,' Saloni said with clenched teeth. Rishabh stepped to form a barrier between them.

'Look guys, we all need to calm down. Akash, I completely understand, you feel betrayed and I'm sorry. This is new and we didn't even know ourselves what it was. It just happened.' Akash held Rishabh by the collar.

'You don't tell me how or what to feel,' Rishabh looked aghast and Saloni's hands shot to cover her face.

'Please let him go. Stop, Akash!' Saloni yelled and begged Akash when she saw him draw a punch. He let go of Rishabh.

'You bastard went behind my back. I trusted you like a brother. Did you sleep with her?'

'That's not your business, Akash! Sorry, but it's your sister we're talking about.' Rishabh's voice was trembling but he maintained his poise.

'You'll pay for this, you bastard. No one goes behind my back. You will pay dearly, because this is my fucking business and I'll ruin your stupid robot to teach you a lesson you'll never forget.'

'What is that supposed to mean, Akash?' Saloni asked confused.

'Shut up. Not a word out of you. Or I'll tell dad everything, you hear me you? Wanna go back to Kolkata on the next flight home? No right? Then keep out of it. And you, get out of my house. From today, it's strictly business and it's about to go bad for you. Mark my words!'

Rishabh was bewildered and hurt listening to his best friend's words. He took a final look at Saloni who was trembling and shaking all over. He threw up his arms in exasperation, turned on his heel and shut the door loudly behind him. This had gone way worse than he had imagined.

How could Akash even think of holding a grudge against me after all this time that we spent together? And he went as far as threatening to ruin the one thing that I've put my heart and soul into! Bawarchi!'

❖

A week flew by. Rishabh had a meeting with his manager to discuss his future endeavors. Everything had gone smoothly, contrary to his imagination. He had finally completed all the software work on Bawarchi, although that took longer than planned, but it had been a productive week.

He met Saloni twice, after her constant insistence. Not that he wasn't interested, but Saloni weirdly expected him to be at her beck and call. All they did when they met was eat scrumptious food at cafés and make out in the washrooms, which rendered Rishabh spent and distracted to focus on anything else for the rest of the day. She too had come over once, unannounced to his place. Rishabh was shocked that she even knew his address, but more so when she introduced herself to his mother as "Rishabh's special friend".

The week had passed without any texts or game invites from Sam. There was a moment every day when he thought of texting her, but his work, Saloni, and other distractions kept him busy. He had still not heard from Akash even after repeatedly trying to get in touch with him. Last night, Rishabh finally decided to let it go and focus on his work. He would handle whatever roadblock Akash threw his way.

After completing all his work for the day, Rishabh sat with a mug of coffee by the window of his living room and finally typed out a text to Sam. He wanted to find out if she was okay after her visit home.

Later that night after dinner, he sent an email to Mr Goenka informing him about the completion of the prototype. A fraction of his mind made him wonder nervously about what would happen if Mr Goenka found out about his affair with Saloni, or if Akash did anything moronic, but he shrugged that thought away.

Just then, Gautam called him. He picked up on the second ring, eager to talk to his friend about the drama that had ensued last week. He told him everything and Gautam was equally shocked when he heard about Akash's threat.

'How did Saloni handle it all? I'm curious,' Gautam asked, intrigued.

'Well, to be honest, I have been doing the "handling" so far. I have tried asking her about how she's able to live under the same roof with a guy who treated her so badly. But every time I ask her she changes the topic by saying she doesn't want to talk about him. I guess they've been staying out of each other's way!'

'Can only imagine how weird that must be,' Gautam responded. 'Are you happy with her?' Gautam asked after a momentary pause.

'What is that supposed to mean, bro? We have only just begun dating.'

'But then why are we in a relationship with someone? It should be something beyond physical attraction and needs, *na*? Like maybe that person makes you feel good about yourself, or adds something valuable to your life. Or maybe, that person spends quality time with you that you wouldn't want to trade for anything ever?'

'Okay, so, then what is your question?'

'It's simple, really. Do you see a future with her?' Rishabh was caught off guard.

'I guess I'll leave you with that thought,'

They said goodbye and Rishabh noticed a string of missed calls on WhatsApp from Saloni. He called back.

'Are you okay?' He asked her.

'Yeah, I'm okay, what would happen to me? I didn't want to make you angry, I just thought you were busy playing that stupid BOA game and were missing my calls,' she said nonchalantly.

'No, Saloni, I was on another call.'

'Oh, with whom?'

'Why is that important?'

'Oh so, it was a girl?'

'What, no! I was talking to Gautam. Why do you have to keep a tab on everything Saloni? It's infuriating sometimes.'

'Wow, someone's in a sour mood!'

'Why don't you let me miss you a little, Saloni?'

'But I'm bored! I can't even go outside, it's so hot today!'

'Why not read something or watch a movie, or just draw or sing, or...'

'Eww! Who reads? I am not interested in books. So boring!'

'Okay then, Saloni I'm sorry but I can't help you.'

'But you're supposed to; it's your one job!' Rishabh was on the verge of losing it again.

'Well it may come as a surprise to you, but I do have a lot on my plate right now!' And no, it's not my job to entertain you,' he said the latter more to himself than to her.

Post dinner, Rishabh was watching a movie and playing BOA simultaneously when he saw Sam online. He invited her for a game and tried chatting with her, but she seemed too focused on the game and hardly responded.

❖

Next morning, Mr Goenka's call graced Rishabh's phone. 'Hello beta, how are you? I have news for you – I'll be flying down to Mumbai in two days. You know, Rishabh, we shouldn't delay this, the sooner the better. I have some more news for you, but we'll talk about it when I'm there.'

'All okay uncle!'

'Yes, again you got serious!' He chortled. 'It's very good news Rishabh! But you will have to wait for it.'

'Sure uncle, let me know when you want to see me.'

'I will,' he took a brief pause then added. 'Is Akash okay?'

'Yes, I think, why what happened?' Rishabh gulped and his throat went suddenly dry.

'Nothing really, he and Saloni have not been taking my calls. Their mom is also worried. So, another reason why I thought of coming so soon. Is everything okay?' he asked somberly.

Rishabh hesitated but tried to assure him that it's all good. 'Maybe Akash is just busy with work or something.'

'Hmm, okay beta. I'll see you soon. Can't wait to meet your brainchild!'

❖

Rishabh had tried to get in touch with Akash multiple times during the last two days. He had even risked his life again and gone to his place to talk it out. But Akash was not at home.

When Rishabh had told her about her dad's call, she had cheered him on, missing the crux. 'Oh baby, I'm so excited for you.'

'I am worried though. What if Akash opens his mouth and vomits everything about us to your dad?'

'Oh no, boo, don't stress. He won't do it. He is your partner after all.'

'Still, he did threaten to hold it as collateral. Can you please try and talk to him when he's back?' Rishabh asked. Saloni rolled her eyes and said nothing.

'Babe, both of us will suffer if he opens his mouth.' Saloni was suddenly startled by that thought. No matter what befalls, she couldn't imagine going back to Kolkata now.

'I'll see what I can do,' she said.

Saloni was able to talk to Akash and ask him not to mention Rishabh and her affair to their dad. She texted Rishabh with the confirmation later that night.

Let's just say, he owed me. Big time! Don't worry about it. Just focus on the meeting now! Miss you!

Rishabh was a little relieved and left a text to Akash.

Bro, I am really grateful to have you by my side. I need my partner tomorrow. I hope we can celebrate whatever good news your dad is bringing our way, together.

❖

Next afternoon, Rishabh headed for Akash's residence, carrying a bottle of whiskey. Mr Goenka had asked him to meet over lunch. Akash was nowhere around. Saloni had gone to lunch with her college friends too, which was something Rishabh already knew. He had suggested that to keep her at a safe distance, in case anything went wrong. Mr Goenka greeted Rishabh and asked Bablu to open the whiskey bottle and get out two glasses. Bablu had prepared a feast for his *sahib* and Rishabh bhaiya.

'Akash bhaiya left for the gym half an hour back, just before Goenka sahib arrived,'

Rishabh had hoped for Akash to be here. Mr Goenka was equally curious to know why both his children were away.

'Forget it! Let us focus on what is more important. You, my genius boy!' He laughed loudly frightening Rishabh a little. His laugh was even more ominous in person.

'Should we wait for Akash, uncle?'

'You can fill him up on this later, maybe at dinner tonight. You're coming with us, remember! So, where is this Bawarchi?'

Over the next twenty minutes Rishabh gave Mr Goenka a brief demo of Bawarchi while explaining its functioning. Mr Goenka looked on with concentration, repeating words that Rishabh uttered to himself, asking no questions. He was taken aback when Bawarchi successfully prepared a bowl of upma right in front of him in just a minute.

'Brilliant beta! This is exactly what I was hoping to see. You have done it!' He hugged Rishabh, surprising him, and patted him loudly on the back. Mr Goenka couldn't take his eyes off the robot and kept analyzing him from various angles.

Hesitantly, he asked, 'Can I hold him?' He smiled like a wonderstruck child when he picked him up.

'Not very heavy, either!' He exclaimed, surprised by the lightness of the robot in his hands. Rishabh explained how he has used microtechnology and mechatronics to keep it lightweight as that would help with shipping. It also helped in avoiding overheating of circuits.

Mr Goenka nodded with his lips puckered, impressed. Rishabh was relieved at how smooth the meeting went. Finally, he started telling Rishabh about the good news – there are two actually.

'First good news, I have received a large order from a corporation that wants to distribute Bawarchi.'

'How large an order?'

'They have asked for 5000 units.'

'5000?' Rishabh's jaw dropped open.

'For the first set of orders. They want to roll out three sets before increasing numbers. I told them we can start delivering in three months' time. You think we can get that many ready in three months'? Or you need more time?'

'I will need a team, and funds to get them all rolling. How…'

'That's where the second and bigger good news comes in,' Mr Goenka interrupted Rishabh's train of thought. 'There is a client of mine, from California, he is an NRI investor who works for T. Mcdowell, Sahil Arora. He wants to invest in your business. We are talking about $5million!'

Rishabh was speechless, his mouth hung open in shock.

'The great news is that he is in India this week and so I invited him out to dinner with us, tonight! You can officially pitch Bawarchi to him over dinner. He is already sold on your idea, just wants to meet you and Bawarchi in person. So, you think you're ready for another meal and meeting?' Mr Goenka placed his hand on Rishabh's shoulder.

'Welcome to your new life, Rishabh beta!' Mr Goenka guffawed and the sheer volume of his laugh got Rishabh out of his shock.

'And don't worry about the contract, beta. After dinner tonight, when everything is finalized, we can get all contracts sorted out together. They should all be ready this week. I will leave only after delivering the contract to you. You have my word.'

❖

Later that night, the party of four found itself at Taj. Rishabh had never stepped foot in the lavish hotel. He was taking in the larger-than-life ambience of the place. The marble reflected the light of the chandeliers and the hotel lobby was resplendent golden.

'There he is. Hello, Sahil!' Mr Goenka called out to the tall man approaching them. He was dressed in a beige dress suit, sporting a hint of stubble. He nodded and greeted Mr Goenka who pulled him in a hug. He introduced Sahil to his kids first and then Rishabh. They both shared a firm handshake, looking calculatedly in each other's eyes.

The evening saw Sahil charm everyone, including Saloni, whom he called a "beautiful princess" as soon as he laid eyes on her. She blushed every time he spoke to her. He had then focussed his attention on Rishabh as they took seats at the table by the window facing the bay. Rishabh was sweating again and wiping his face quite ungraciously with the napkin.

'Take it easy, Rishabh. No need to put undue pressure on yourself, buddy. I am already sold on your product. I am ready to bid even more, whatever number you like. This product deserves to be in the market, as soon as today, if only that could happen.'

'Thank you, Mr Arora, I...'

'Oh, just call me Sahil.'

'Thank you for believing in our product.'

'Our?'

'Yes, Akash is my partner,'

'Oh, I didn't know. What fine geniuses we are in the midst of!' The acknowledgement made Akash look up at Rishabh for the first time tonight.

'Well, cheers to both of you then! Let's get some champagne for the table. Would you care to choose a bottle,' he said to Saloni handing her the drinks menu, who giggled softly, constantly blushing.

Rishabh felt amused looking at this. The champagne arrived and Sahil toasted – 'To the bright minds at this table! For letting me be a part of this journey.' They all clunked their champagne flutes and took a swig. Saloni was already down two glasses and Akash was finally starting to speak.

Sahil then asked Rishabh if he had ever been to California.

'No, I wish. I do have a friend though. She lives there.'

Saloni became alert at the mention of a "friend". She looked at Rishabh but dropped it when she sensed her dad's eyes on her. Dinner finally came to an end after some great food and repartee. Sahil invited himself to Akash's place the next day, hoping to see Bawarchi in the flesh and sealing the deal.

The first half of the next day had gone well for Rishabh. After seeing the demo at the Goenka residence, Sahil had jumped the gun and talked about how the project was capable of generating a lot of buzz in the market if put to test right away. Sahil had asked them if he could keep Bawarchi with him for a couple days. Mr Goenka had agreed but the final verdict lay with Rishabh, who suddenly couldn't think of any reasons to ignore Sahil's request.

Things had flowed utterly smoothly one after the other ever since Mr Goenka came to town. Akash hadn't blabbered anything to his dad too!

Rishabh certainly had not expected this level of maturity from him. He owed him. He decided to patch things up with Akash as soon as Mr Goenka left town. Since so much was happening in his life, he couldn't help but text Sam.

'Hey Cali girl, what's up with you?' This time around she instantly replied with a "hey" and "nothing much".

'How was the your week? Were you not well the last time we spoke?'

'No, I was just stressed about something, work related. I had this interview yesterday at Quincy Jones, so I was simply thinking about everything that could go wrong.'

'How did it go then? I'm sure you must have hit it out of the park, but still.'

'Well it did go better than I had expected, but can't say anything. Apparently, they've been interviewing for the position for almost a week now and they called in around ten people on the day I went in. So, the odds aren't that great.'

'You're overthinking again! Just stop fussing over it. I'm sure you did your best, See, all you can do is wait and hope that even if you don't get this, there's some great lesson you learn, right?'

'Anyway, enough about me. How was your week?' She decided not to mention the date night, she couldn't tell how she'd react if he talked about his girlfriend.

'Well, it was better than great. It obviously started off on a high note, all thanks to you. So, don't think I forgot my promise! Next time you're in Mumbai or I'm in LA, I'm taking you on that date I promised! ;-)'

Sam felt her heart flutter and her cheeks turned red. Thankfully nobody could see her and Rishabh continued. 'But the end is looking even better.'

'Really? How?'

Rishabh typed out a small recap of his meeting with Mr Goenka and the good news that he brought with him.

'So, not only am I already getting orders, I even have an angel investor! And guess where he's from?'

'Don't say, California?' Sam quipped.

'That's right!'

'Oh my god, that's great news, Rishabh!'

'Wait for it! He has offered to invest five million dollars! Is that great or what?'

Sam rubbed her eyes. 'That's great, dude! You're going to be a millionaire! Wow, is he a big shot? If he's from around here and an investor, I guess I might know him or he may be my client, you know, from when I worked at T. Mcdowell.'

'Wait, you were at T. Mcdowell? He actually still works there.'

'Really? Who could it be?' Samira had a hunch it was someone she knew, but not someone she worked in such close proximity with.

'It's Sahil Arora,'

Sam couldn't breathe.

'Do you know him?'

This cannot be happening. Why was Sahil interested in Rishabh's product? Did he know about how she'd been texting Rishabh?

She had to put her phone away to go and splash some water on her face in the bathroom. She looked at her reflection and gulped down a glass of cold water. He had almost ruined one life; she wouldn't let him ruin another.

She picked up her phone again. Rishabh had left behind a string of "??????".

'Yes, of course, I know him. Sahil Arora was my boyfriend.'

It had taken every ounce of her strength to type that last sentence. It felt as though she was a recovered addict who was being forced to fall back into intemperance. However, one thing she was certain about. Sahil was a bad guy, one could always count on him to have a motive. All she could do was warn Rishabh by showing him Sahil's true face.

She waited for Rishabh to return, but used the empty minutes to fill him on what she had gone through with Sahil. She briefly told him about how Sahil abused her and how he was one of the major reasons she had called it quits at her previous job, without going into too many details.

Rishabh texted a few minutes later after having absorbed all this information.

'Samira, I don't know what to say. I definitely believe you. You don't have to scrape old wounds, it's pointless. But do you think he has a motive? Mr Goenka seems to know him and trust him quite fervently.'

Sam jumped to pick up her phone as soon as it buzzed. She noticed that it was the first time that he had called her by her full name and that oddly felt good.

'How long have you known this Mr Goenka? Don't get me wrong, I know he's your friend's dad, but people can be untrustworthy, no offense!'

'Not long actually. I have been friends with Akash for some years but Mr Goenka is just an acquaintance.' He thought hard about this.

'So, are you saying that they are duping me? But why would they? I don't see how they would benefit from this?'

'Look! I'm not drawing any conclusions, but *Sahil* cannot be trusted. If I've learnt anything from my past work and personal relationship with him, it's that. I don't know about this Mr Goenka. But I'd say be careful and keep your eyes and ears open. You surely must have the patents and the robot itself, so nothing bad should happen. I wouldn't want to see you or even my worst enemy getting associated with that pig, Arora!'

Rishabh's eyes protruded with disbelief.

'Actually, I haven't filed the patents yet, and I just handed over Bawarchi to Sahil and Mr Goenka to get him ready for pitches for the rest of the week.'

'What! You got to be kidding me! Do something!'

Rishabh felt angry at himself yet there was no way of knowing if he was being set up for impending doom.

Wait! Maybe Akash knows something about it. Was this something he conspired along with the other two players just to teach me a lesson?

14

Antivirus

Rishabh rang the bell outside Goenka's residence, impatiently shaking his leg and brushing the nape of his neck. 'Open up!' He said out loudly, out of frustration.

Akash came out of his room yawning.

'What the hell is happening here?' He asked with a perplexed expression. Rishabh jogged up to him.

'Bro, I need you to answer something. Is Sahil here to steal the robot and our entire venture?'

'What?' Akash asked, rubbing his eyes.

'Tell me the truth, Akash!' This time around, it was Rishabh curling his fists. Saloni couldn't believe what she was looking at.

'I have no clue what you're talking about!'

'Okay, so you don't know Sahil?'

'No, I just met him the other day, with you.'

Rishabh grasped his head with both hands, exasperated.

'What's wrong, bro?' Akash asked. Rishabh told him about Sam's warning without name-dropping her. Akash stayed quiet.

'Wait a minute! Are you accusing my dad of fraud? That's real big of you, Rishabh. First my sister. Now my dad? Next, you'll say I robbed you!'

Rishabh tried to calm Akash down. 'Bro, I'm really scared. This is something I have been working towards for years now! I'm not saying it's your dad. But Sahil is definitely a stranger with a suspicious record! It also doesn't help that my entire tech is with them and I'm here without any patents or a written contract to prove my intellectual ownership over anything!' Rishabh stopped mid-rant to take a deep breath.

'I came to you for seeking help, not to accuse your dad of anything. Please Akash, if you know something, tell me.'

Akash went to his room to get his mobile phone. Saloni inched closer to Rishabh to pat his arm. Akash came back, signaling them both to stay quiet as he put his phone on speaker.

'Hey dad, yeah, I'm good. I wanted to ask you if the contract's already been written up. If it's still in process, can my share be increased to 30% instead of 25%? You know I'm not talking to Rishabh so, I thought I'd ask the real investor. Would Sahil be okay with it? Rishabh doesn't have to know right now, dad. Can you keep this between us?'

Mr Goenka's voice reverberated across the silent living room. 'Arre beta, if you say I'll give you a 100%! After all, what's mine is yours, Akash. Also, keep this between us – Sahil has a great plan. He got the meeting arranged with the overseas investors for tomorrow evening. The meeting will be a success once we give them the demo and the project will be worth multi-million dollars! I was smart enough to keep Rishabh hanging, but Sahil needs to take the robot out of here soon for the deal to work. I can get it manufactured here for a very cheap rate, ship it all to Sahil and he can sell and give us 70% of the profits. The gains will belong to you and your sister.'

Saloni's mouth hung open and Akash put a finger on his lips again, gesturing her to stay silent.

'Wow dad! I've got to give it to you, brilliant plan!' He disconnected after assuring his dad that he wouldn't utter a word to Rishabh.

Rishabh's fears were true. Saloni came closer to hug him and he forcibly pushed her hand away. Offended, Saloni strutted to her room, loudly banging the door behind her.

Akash broke the silence. 'Bro, I'm sorry I didn't trust you. I knew my dad was a wolf, but this is more like a hyena,' He felt angry at himself.

After a brief pause he added, 'What am I supposed to do? He never mentioned where the meeting would be.'

'Even if we knew, how would we stop them?' Rishabh said, shaking his head in disbelief. He was suddenly cold and shivering. Akash put a hand over his shoulder.

'Hey, I'm sorry about this. I wish I was with you these last few weeks.'

'Well, I need you now,' Rishabh said.

'What's done is done. And I am with you! I'll do my best to support you. Although if I pester my dad about the meeting venue, it could raise doubts in his head. You know, if he trusts me, he'll keep divulging information that we could use.'

'But we need something now! If that meeting tomorrow goes well, we can say goodbye to Bawarchi forever.'

What seemed like an hour passed away swiftly, with neither concrete plans nor any boosted spirits.

'Maybe uncle can help?' Akash suggested.

'How can he without any hard proof, bro?' They both stood up stiffly and took a deep breath right as Saloni came out of her room angrily.

'So, you're going? And you'll talk to this guy but not me? Or did you not realize how badly you treated me a few minutes back?'

'Saloni please, this is really not the time...'

'Oh yeah, is it not convenient for *you* to talk to your girlfriend right now?'

Akash quietly walked back to his room, sensing the looming anger in the living room.

'Yes, exactly. It's anything but convenient. And have you ever stopped to consider being a supportive friend to me instead of this annoying girlfriend?' Rishabh was clearly losing his patience.

'Oh, so now Akash is a supportive friend but when you want to have fun, you come running to me!'

'I come running to you?' Rishabh snickered which angered Saloni even more.

'Don't you dare laugh at me!'

'I can't take this anymore. I have enough on my plate!'

'What is that supposed to mean?' she hesitated.

'I can't do *this*,' He gestured at the space between them with his hands animatedly.

Saloni immediately broke down. 'I'm sorry, what did I do? She came closer and caressed his face. I've upset you now.' He took her hands off his face.

'No, Saloni, this is not working out. I really cannot focus on you or this relationship right now, with the troubles that your dad has created for me. I need some time. It's better for us both.' He brushed her hair and walked away.

❖

That night, sleep evaded Rishabh. He kept tossing and turning in his bed, with his thoughts overwhelming him. His mom had failed to keep her emotions at bay when he broke the news to his parents. His dad was surprisingly quiet; he was probably trying to think of a loophole himself. Rishabh finally gave up on sleep and sat up in bed.

He felt a strange urgency to talk to Sam. *What would she be doing right now?* He logged onto BOA, in the hope to bump into Sam and talk to her. He noticed her online and immediately sent her an invite. She accepted and they both remained silent for a minute, focussing on the game, Rishabh's avatar was causing havoc on the screen.

'Umm! Hey, Rishabh?' Sam asked, a little horrified from the aggressive bloodbath. She knew his game style and this was definitely not it.

'Hi, how are you,' he exclaimed awkwardly. He paused a little and waved slightly towards Swan.

She waved back. 'Are you okay? What's wrong?' Sam sounded genuinely concerned.

'So, I took your advice and spoke to Akash and turns out you were right!'

Sam broke the awkward, intermittent silence. 'Oh boy! I'm so sorry Rishabh. It is unfortunate that you had to even cross paths with that swine! Umm...what can you do?' Sam said, thinking of solutions. 'I'm sure there's a way out,' she said with her forehead creased in utter concentration.

Just then, it hit her.

'Okay, Mr problem solver! How did you forget your own theory?' she asked excitedly.

'My theory?'

'Yes, why don't you run an antivirus program to drive out the virus?' Rishabh could hear her smile over the phone.

'Antivirus, eh? What could it be?' All this time he was so focused on stopping the people involved that he totally forgot to see the other side.

'Antivirus,' he repeated again, with more resolve. 'I have the tamper controls!' he almost yelled with realization.

'There you go!' Samira egged him on.

The thought finally occurred to him – I *can shut it all down! Nobody would want to invest in a flop show!* The idea had a snowball effect on Rishabh's brain. He couldn't stop envisaging the entire action plan that lay ahead of him.

Rishabh was ecstatic. The clouds had finally parted and he could think clearly.

'Swan! I don't know what I'd do without you! You are my hero!'

'Yeah yeah, tell me something new,' she felt happy having helped Rishabh.

He suddenly went silent and stopped listening, his mind now elsewhere.

'Hello? Am I still talking to the biggest nerd on Earth?' Rishabh came out of his daydream. 'Sorry, I lost you. What were you saying?'

'Geez, I just rambled on an entire paragraph! Where are you lost? Thinking about the girlfriend?' Sam instantly regretted her childish question and bit her lip.

'Haha, no, definitely not thinking about *her*! Also, she's not my girlfriend anymore,' he said.

'Oh, what?' she declared with genuine surprise.

'Saloni isn't my girlfriend anymore. We broke up. I ended it,' he said it out aloud, for the first time.

'Oh. What happened? Actually, no, you don't need to tell me. Sorry for intruding.'

'No, it's okay. We really need to stop with the formalities, Swan!' he playfully scolded her. 'What don't we know about each other, really?' He began telling her about how he'd lost his cool and broken up with Saloni.

Maybe this was a sign, a voice in her head told her. Tell him, it tried to persuade her. Tell him now, Sam!

'Well, there is one little thing that you don't know about me,' she blurted out.

'And that is?' He didn't add a "if you want to tell me".

'So, you know how I'm kind of jobless right now and still waiting to hear back from some companies, while interviews with others are still in the pipeline. My grandmother has not been keeping well since the last couple months, and mom really wants to go see her. She has been begging us all to come and meet her soon, you know how old people get, emotional blackmailing and all. My aunt told us she's much better now, but mom has just made up her mind, especially now that I have no option but to tag along with them. So, I'll be visiting my Nani,'

'That's...good?' he sounded confused. Sam quickly went over what she'd just told him. 'Oh, I missed out a detail. My Nani lives in Mumbai!'

'Wait, you're coming to *Mumbai*? *Swan*!! That's *great* news! When?' He sounded out of breath.

'Chill, breathe. I'll be flying down in about three weeks' time.'

'WE HAVE TO MEET SWAN!'

Sam couldn't help but laugh at Rishabh's reaction to her news.

Finally relieved, Rishabh fired up his laptop and activated the tamper controls on Bawarchi. He crossed his fingers and squeezed his eyes shut, hoping for everything to work as per his plan.

❖

At the meeting with investors that evening, Mr Goenka and Sahil had talked up the robot and finally revealed Bawarchi.

'And finally, the genius in the flesh – Ultimate Chef,' Sahil called out, unveiling the robot. They had rebranded Bawarchi as "Ultimate Chef" to appeal to the US market and also because it was easier for them to pronounce. They all looked eagerly at the robot. Mr Goenka switched it on and put some ingredients in. But Bawarchi stood motionless, no whirring sounds, no lights glowing. There was no sign to tell if Bawarchi was working. He awkwardly smiled and Sahil got up to fix it, to no avail.

'Let's just give it a few seconds. Sahil, can you restart it please?' Mr Goenka said, smiling gawkily. Why wasn't it working? Sahil turned the robot on and off about ten times before banging it loudly on the table out of anger.

'Sorry, we are facing some issues it seems,' Mr Goenka called out to the investors on the other side of the screen again.

'Are you sure it works without banging it on the table? One of the investors joked and they all laughed. Sahil lost it then and walked out of the room, leaving the robot lying upside down on the table. 'This is what I was putting in a million bucks for? What a waste of time!' Mr Goenka partially smiled and apologized.

'Call us when your robot wakes up!' They disconnected the call. The pitch was a huge disaster and Mr Goenka sat with his head in his hands.

The news had reached Rishabh and Akash through a conference call from Mr Goenka. Sahil had decided to back out and Mr Goenka too seemed dubious about the whole thing.

'Beta, I think it needs more work. You can't think of selling a product that only works around you!'

'Yes uncle, you're right.'

15
Trouble in paradise?

Rishabh, with his dad's help, was successful in filing patents for Bawarchi, along with retrieving the physical robot back from Mr Goenka's possession. Ever since the fiasco, Rishabh had absolutely no time for anything or anyone else.

Right after bringing Bawarchi home, he had deactivated the tamper controls and tried to switch the robot back to life. And thankfully, it had all worked out well.

After a few days, Rishabh had decided to meet Akash. Things were slowly getting back to normal between them. Mr Goenka had left town a couple days back. Akash had to act like he was very angry at the state of affairs.

'So, how are things now? Is uncle still mad at you?' Akash asked.

'Can you blame him? But he's okay, he'll come around in a few days. Mom's handling that side of things and I am focusing on getting Bawarchi off his feet soon. Can't stop to think about anything else right now. I just thought I'd come see you for a bit, needed to get out of the house too,'

After a pause Akash said, 'I am sorry, I know it doesn't change anything. But I want you to know that I will never doubt you. I am ashamed of what my father did to you.'

'You don't have to be sorry, Akash. Please chill bro, it's all okay.'

Anyway, one last thing. I want to put in some money…'

'No Akash, please, no more money! If I've learnt any lesson from this entire fiasco, it's to not mix friendship with money, especially not your dad's! I will not accept any money from you or any of my friends,'

'Then how can I help you?' Akash asked with every ounce of sincerity within him.

Rishabh looked at him kindly for a moment and said, 'By just being yourself. By lifting me up and boosting my confidence when I need it the most. That's it. And besides, I have been working on something to raise money for Bawarchi.'

'Well I wish you luck with it and I'm sure something great will come out of it.'

Just then, the door unlocked from outside and Saloni stepped in, sweaty, with her hair tied up in a high ponytail, in neon pink shorts, hot pink Nike sneakers, and an oversized white t-shirt. She was looking into her phone, humming a song, her ears plugged with headphones. She froze in her tracks as soon as she looked up and saw Rishabh.

'Hi,' she said nonchalantly as she resumed her march to the kitchen to pick up a bottle of water from the fridge. She took a big gulp from the bottle and started walking to her room. She hesitated briefly around the living room and then exclaimed with a sigh, 'how are you Rishabh? Can we talk?'

He nodded, taken aback by this sudden confrontation. She smiled sweetly at him and walked over to her room, leaving the door ajar.

As soon as he entered her room, Saloni embraced him in a hug, her face against his chest, breathing in his scent.

'I've missed you, Rish!' She smiled and sighed. He let her be for a couple seconds, then gently freed himself of her.

'Yeah, it's been long, hasn't it!'

'A week and some more,' she said, untying her hair and letting it fall over her shoulders and back. She was flushed from her workout at the gym. Rishabh was staring at her but deflected his attention and cleared his throat.

'It's okay, you can stare. I know you like it.' She stepped towards him again, interlacing her fingers with his. 'I like it too.'

He stepped back. 'No Saloni, this is wrong. In case you forgot, we broke up.'

'But that was because you were going through a difficult time! But now things are fine, right? We can try being together again. I miss you. Don't you miss me, babe?'

'I do miss you, Saloni, but for completely different reasons. I am still pretty involved with my robot. That's all I am thinking about right now, honestly.' Her face tightened.

'Look, please don't take this personally, I...' Rishabh tried to explain himself but was interrupted by Saloni

'There's someone else, isn't there? I had a feeling you were seeing someone behind my back. Or did you find someone on Hot or Not in the last week?'

'Where's this coming from, Saloni? And no! I am not seeing anyone else. Jeez, this is exactly why this didn't work!' He steadied his voice that was now quivering with irritation and anger.

Saloni rushed to hug him again and said, 'I'm sorry, babe, please don't be mad. I'll try to be better, you'll see. I just don't want this to end.'

He gently patted her head. 'But it's already done, Saloni. I'm not mad, sorry for yelling. But, you don't have to be better. Look, you have to get over this obsession of changing yourself for other people. You're already pretty good.' He moved her to look at her face.

'You are enough to be loved by someone who respects and loves you the way you are. Maybe that's not me. I really feel that if we jumped into anything again, it would be devastating for both of us. Isn't it better if we end things this way? We'll stay friends, if you like? And I'm always here for you.'

She held his hand close to her face. 'You think we can't make it work, but you're wrong. I know I love you, and you do too. I'll support you wholeheartedly. Is it because my dad bluffed that you're taking it out on me now?'

'No! That has nothing to do with this. Please listen to me, Saloni!'

'No, there's definitely a way out, if we both try.'

'But I don't want to try.' he said a little too strongly, freeing his hand.

To evade any further drama, Rishabh went out of the room. He had left his phone on the bed which caught Saloni's eye and she pounced on it. She sat on the bed and quickly traced the screen lock pattern that she had memorized.

She quickly tapped on the WhatsApp logo and screened his contacts – right then she saw a name that sounded familiar – Sam LA. The conversation from the dinner at Taj came back to her.

So, he is talking to this bitch. I was right. She muttered to herself. She read the messages and started shaking with anger.

In a moment of pure anger, she typed out a nasty message to her.

Yo bitch! Go tell your sob story to someone who actually cares! Stop bothering my boyfriend, he has enough on his plate than to type out sympathy messages to another hoe out there! In plain words – fuck off.

That should teach her.

❖

Sam was cradling a warm cup of hot chocolate in her hands when her phone beeped loudly. Her eyes, reading through the interview notes on her laptop screen, were on the brink of closing when that loud buzz awakened her.

Who is it so late? She thought to herself. She saw Rishabh's name and something lit up inside her. As soon as she read the words crawling on the dimly lit screen, a hoarse breath escaped her mouth. She felt like someone had punched her hard in the gut. She took a sharp breath and curled her hands into fists, so tight that they turned white.

'What the fuck,' she muttered to herself with gritted teeth. Her eyes were filled with tears,

Neha was right, I should know better by now. She dropped the cup of hot chocolate hard onto the floor and a sob escaped her trembling lips.

No, I won't cry over a stupid message like this. I can really live without the drama! She thought Rishabh was her friend. That made her chortle.

Friend! Wow, it's like I was living under a rock. A part of her brain tried to convince her that it was his stupid girlfriend. All this time she thought only he was privy to their messages but this girl had obviously read them all.

'He told me he had broken up with her. That liar!' That angered her more.

She scrolled up to read their last conversation and ended feeling even more wrath at this stranger who had chosen to breach their privacy . She put her phone down and rubbed her face dry. She sniffled and picked it up again only to block Rishabh's number from her phone. She set it down and almost got up to clean the mess beside her when a thought struck her. She picked her phone again and opened BOA. She blocked him from there too.

❖

After the struggle to acquire the rights of Bawarchi ended in triumph, Rishabh decided to launch a Kickstarter campaign just as Sam had suggested about a month. The campaign was simple – a descriptive video showing Bawarchi's strengths and a meaningful interview of Rishabh talking about his journey of creating the robot.

In order to jumpstart the campaign, Rishabh engaged in some influencer marketing and some paid advertising initially, but soon after that, the reach skyrocketed and funds were flowing in from around the world.

In less than three weeks, the campaign had surpassed its goal of raising $50,000 and continued to gain momentum and cross $100,000. Rishabh started receiving messages from eager backers from France, UK, South Korea and the United States. People couldn't wait to receive their shipment and he committed to fulfilling it in few months.

Word of his endeavor had even reached news agencies and new media handles on Instagram, who wanted to run features on him and his inspiring entrepreneurial journey so far. These things made Rishabh feel exhilarated but he was always on guard. Rishabh had learned his lessons the hard way. Never again was he going to spill all beans or believe anyone at face value. His friends and family began sending him pictures of his features in their local newspapers and screenshots of his digital interviews. This time around, something good was definitely coming his way; he could feel it in his bones.

Finally, Rishabh was able to handle things better; he found time to talk to his friends and socialize. Discussing his friends' higher education plans had inevitably made Rishabh think about it and he had been staying up nights looking through college e-brochures and registering to attend a few higher education fairs in Mumbai later that month.

It was a day or two before her visit to India when Rishabh thought of reaching out to Sam and thanking her for all the help.

'I should've done it sooner, but it's not too late, right? Can't wait to celebrate with her in person,' he said to himself.

Rishabh opened his gaming app and scrolled down to her profile, but as he neared closer to it, he observed a bright red sign near the name Brown Swan.

'Wait a second, she's blocked?' He kept scrolling up and down to see if any other names were blocked too. But the bright red circle with a clear white line cut in its middle struck out on his phone screen.

How did I not catch this before? He thought hard, trying to refresh his memory.

'Did I block her by mistake? Did my fingers slip and hit the block button on the screen?' he said to himself.

But suddenly Saloni's questions came rushing back to his mind *Who is Sam? Are you seeing someone else? Was it a girl?*

'Oh man, it's got to be Saloni!' he exclaimed, pulling at his hair. He was still living with the after-effects of having dated her.

He unblocked her and sent her a message, immediately trying to salvage the situation. 'I need to fix this, but I can't reach out to Saloni, not now at least.' He shuddered even thinking about their last confrontation.

He waited a few minutes contemplating his next move and decided to send another message.

Hey! I'm so sorry I didn't know that you were blocked! It must've been Saloni, remember my toxic ex? Anyway, you'll never believe what happened with my robot, it's a story worth celebrating in person! You're still coming here in a couple days, right? Please text me when you get here! Can't wait to see you!

And then, the waiting game resumed. He checked his gaming app every hour. But, he received no response. By the end of the first day, Rishabh couldn't hold it any longer. He texted her again and again. There must be another way!

Then, it hit him like a bullet – WhatsApp! As soon as he opened up the chat window, the last message from him to Saloni caught his eyes. In her hurry, Saloni had forgotten to delete the crude message she had typed out before blocking Sam. Rishabh couldn't believe his eyes. He definitely knew whose words he was reading again and again. He threw his phone beside him on the bed and lay back, massaging his eyes and forehead.

'What did you do, Saloni!' he yelled. If anything, he was angrier at himself for leaving his phone unattended around her.

'Now I know why she "understood" me.' He played with the idea of calling her up and hurling abuses at her, but soon decided against it.

'What difference does it make now,' he said dejectedly as he got up.

He tried texting Sam but his messages could not get delivered, she was blocked here too.

'Of course, Saloni did one thing right, I guess,' He quickly unblocked her and texted again, this time typing out a profuse apology. He shook his head dejectedly after sending the message and clicked his phone away again.

❖

Two days later, Rishabh's anxiety began to heighten and he decided to sleuth further. None of her messages had been successful in receiving a reply from Sam.

What other way do I have to reach her? Oh wait, why am I sitting here waiting when I can look for her on social media! He jumped up at his workstation and quickly began scanning all social media platforms.

'She could have a Soundcloud profile too.' He muttered to himself as he continued surfing half a dozen websites in the pursuit of finding her. He spent the rest of his night trying to look for her, but not having her last name was turning out to be a real challenge.

It was while he was busy surfing on Facebook when it occurred to him – *I know how she looks! Of course, that picture she had uploaded of herself a few months back!*

Inspired, he sat tracking all profiles named Samira on Facebook, filtering through location. After forty odd minutes, Eureka! He found her! He quickly sent her a friend request.

What if she's mad at me and doesn't accept my request? Might have to take the creepy guy route for this one – if I can find a way into her "Other Messages" folder.

He was in a strange dilemma that made him feel anxious and laugh in the same instant. He typed a long apology and let her know that he was really sorry about how her ex-girlfriend behaved with her.

I cannot take back that message, but I can certainly hope to repair some of the collateral damage. He crossed his fingers and hit send.

For the next four days, there was no response. Rishabh was now wondering if Sam would even respond after all the drama that had ensued as a result of Saloni's antics. That night as he was surfing through Facebook, he hit refresh on Sam's profile. He kept hitting refresh after every few seconds.

Every time Sam's profile picture loaded up on his screen, Rishabh tried to memorize one little feature that he had not before noticed– first her eyes, light brown and almond shaped, then the sharp tip of her long nose, her nose ring, her lips – the peak of her cupid's bow and her bottom lip plump in the center, her pale cheeks, spotted with pink close to her eyes, her jet-black hair, a side bang falling across one of her heavily kohl-rimmed eyes. He tried to retain her face at the back of his eyelids as they were shut, pulling him in, deeper and deeper into sleep.

Later, he woke up with a jolt. It had been quite sometime since he was trying to get in touch with Sam now.

I don't think this is going to work anymore.

❖

A day after receiving that boorish message from Saloni, Sam's interview had gone well, but nothing much had come out of it so far. Nothing, barring her candid chat with the executive producer of the studio that she interviewed with, which had culminated into them exchanging their contact information with each other. She was sure to follow-up on the conversation properly, once her India trip was done.

Sam had not once thought about the message or regretted blocking Rishabh since the night before, and was now focusing all her energy and attention on helping her parents pack and prepare for their forthcoming trip.

Two days later, she had packed everything and made her way to their place in Irvine.

Things were good. Her parents kept busy, organizing their luggage and forcefully feeding her. And then, she used to practise on her drum set in the basement for close to an hour every day. She had suddenly found surplus hours to spend with Neha. She had carefully avoided the subject of Rishabh but Neha had gone ahead and asked her whether she had told him about her visit. Sam had casually admonished the topic away with a 'yeah I may have mentioned something ages back when the plan was still fresh.'

'So, will you meet him then? Have you guys planned anything?' Neha threw Sam a cautionary look who knew this question was coming all along.

'Oh, please no! We've hardly been talking.' Sam maintained a cool tone.

'Oh, did something happen?' Neha asked, her voice laced with genuine concern.

'No, nothing really! Guess we just got busy with our respective lives. He has a girlfriend anyway and I didn't want to get in the middle of anything complicated. Plus, he's not your dictionary definition of a "matured guy".' Sam stopped her rant at midway as Neha looked probingly into her eyes.

'What?' Sam demanded and looked away.

'Nothing, just checking if you're telling me the truth. You're okay, right?'

'Yes, mommy!' Sam shot her a fake grin and laughed.

16
Missed Connections

It was finally the day of Sam's flight to India. Her family was flying from LAX to Istanbul to Mumbai and the transit time was supposed to be twenty-two hours. Rishabh had tried reaching her today, but she was unaware as she had blocked him on BOA and WhatsApp.

The early morning November sky of Mumbai was clear blue and it was the right degree of warm. Sam's uncle and cousins had come to pick them up from the airport. They all greeted each other like long-lost friends; there was hugging and crying.

She felt weird embracing people she had barely met, let alone shed tears of joy at seeing their faces after four long years.

'She's grown so big,' her uncle exclaimed. 'She's almost as tall as me,' he said and laughed.

'I think I stopped growing physically about a few years back,' Sam said with a straight face leaving her uncle and dad in splits as her mom stared pointedly at her.

The scene at her grandma's house was pretty similar. Her mom had leapt off the ground at record speed to go and embrace her grandma who was basking in the morning sun, smiling and waving at them. After what felt like hours of waterworks, grabbing faces, kissing foreheads, unsolicited *ashirwads*, and a plethora of comments from every member of the house about how weak they had become, they barely got a few minutes to freshen up when a smorgasbord of homemade delicacies were served.

The house was in Juhu, overlooking the sea, and Sam felt a strange sense of homesickness. She was more tired from the social awkwardness rather than the flight itself. But now she was expected to stuff her face with different homemade snacks. She excused herself and went to her room where she dissolved into deep, uninterrupted sleep.

When she woke up, it was already dusky outside and the house had grown dark and quiet. Around 10 p.m. the next day, her phone lit up – it was a friend request from Rishabh.

Sam hadn't been on Facebook in the last several months and was about to sweep the message off her screen when she read his name. She was still pretty angry when she clicked on the notification. Looking at his profile picture calmed and infuriated her in the same instant. She began sifting through her notifications and messages when she came across Rishabh's text. She spent an entire minute reading the long and convoluted apology after which she exited the app and shut her phone away.

No drama, no drama! She repeated the words like a mantra and buried her head in the pillows on her new bed.

After five days of sleeping almost all day long, walking along the neighboring coastline and stuffing her face with more and more food, Sam couldn't help but think about Rishabh's apology. Every night, when she was all by herself in her room, she opened the message from Rishabh and put her phone away a minute later. After a few minutes she would get up and type a reply or two, before she changed her mind and deleted it away instead of hitting send. Something inexplicable was stopping her.

On the sixth morning, she woke up with a decision. She would take this slow and reply to Rishabh's message. If he was telling the truth, and if he did mean every word of what he had written, she would give him a chance to mend it

❖

When Rishabh saw his phone, he jumped with joy upon seeing that Samira had accepted his friend request. He texted her once again, asking her if she was still around in Mumbai and if they could meet.

I am so happy and relieved that you responded in some way, Sam. I thought I had lost you. I cannot lose you, you're too precious. If it wasn't for you, I would have never got out of that shady deal. If you hadn't warned me about Sahil, I don't know what much I could have done. And I'm really sorry about the whole Saloni thing too. She had no right to say anything to you or go snooping behind my back, especially after our breakup.

I am truly sorry. I wish I could reverse it. I swear, I'll make it up to you if and when we meet! I should have reached out sooner, I know. But just give me one chance, Sam,

An hour later, Sam's message was waiting for Rishabh.

I don't know, Rishabh. You do sound very sorry; you've said it a dozen times. But I don't know if I want to partake in the drama anymore. So, I'll take your apology, but that's it. I'm glad I could help you. Anyway, I'm leaving for LA tonight. I'm already at the airport. Good luck with everything!

Rishabh was shattered. He couldn't believe he had missed his chance.

In an attempt to sound unmoved and unaffected, he typed out a somber, 'Oh okay'. He had hoped his apology would have been enough, his messages would have been enough, his feelings and their friendship would have been enough.

But in the end, all he could make himself say was "okay". It wasn't like he could change anything now; he had no right to ask her to change her plans. This wasn't a movie! Sam's family was in India to see her grandmother. Now that was done and they were headed back to their life, miles away from here. He had sensed her discomfort in the few words that she had typed. Not wanting to end the conversation on such a despondent note, he typed out a last text.

I wish we could have met. I really was looking forward to this, Sam. But no harm! I guess it wasn't meant to be. Wish you a pleasant trip back! Safe travels!' He quickly typed and kept his phone aside.

Morning came, but the memory remained. Rishabh woke up the next day, not wanting to move, his muscles felt like they had atrophied overnight. He was lying on his stomach when his mother entered his room.

'What's wrong Rishabh? You didn't come to the table for breakfast this morning. I called out to you. Are you unwell?' His mom asked, walking over to him and placing her warm hand on his forehead in order to check his temperature.

'No mom, I don't have a fever,' he said cupping her hand before gently removing it from his forehead. Still holding her hand in both of his he said, 'I'm just feeling a little tired. I'll be back to normal in a bit.' He gave her a weak smile. 'I just need to rest,' he said finally, with a hoarse voice as he tried to sit down.

Rishabh spent most part of the morning simply staring out of his bedroom's window – watching birds that perched on his window sill. He hadn't touched his phone ever since he woke up. There was no reason to. He knew nobody had texted or called him.

At least, the person he most wanted to hear from. He felt agitated; why was he getting so affected? Sam's trip to India was just a rare occurrence!

What if her grandma was living in some other city? They still couldn't have met. She had forgiven him, hadn't she?

But something felt amiss. True, he was excited and really keen to see her, but it's not like they had a deal, or they were best friends, or he was in love with her. There was a moment when he felt like picking up the phone and giving Saloni a piece of his mind. This was all her fault, she never understood the limits of privacy or the perils of overstepping.

Even after their breakup she had never given up a chance to make a snide remark at him whenever he visited Akash.

'I can't, I really don't have the energy to talk to her, and not like it's going to make any difference!' It was a strange experience – one wherein he knew what was causing him to feel so disturbed, and yet being unable to do anything about it.

Rishabh was lying motionless in bed when his phone lit up and buzzed. He didn't look at it. But when the phone kept buzzing one message after another, irritated, he picked it up to see who it was from.

'Sam!'

He quickly sat up in bed to read her messages on Facebook.

Look, I feel weird for doing this. I am still in India, for another day at least, that's all I am telling you. You have to understand how sad that message made me – from your girlfriend – ex or current, I really couldn't care less! Sorry that sounded way ruder than I intended it to,

That last one made Rishabh laugh with relief. There was still some hope of reconciliation.

I think I could spare an hour and meet you; if that's something you still want.

Rishabh had been awake since morning, but only now he was wide awake. His fingers started typing as soon as they touched his phone.

That's really big of you, Sam! And I am truly sorry for her behavior. And yes, I would love to meet you! A big grin had replaced the hours of despair on his face.

17
Naturally Yours

Their "date" venue was only a short walk away from Sam's temporary abode and she chose to walk. What she hadn't accounted for was the humidity that made her tresses stand up with frizz and cover her face and neck in sweat.

'Ugh what is with this city and its weather!'

She tied up her hair in a quick bun right before reaching the café. She had heard about the place but never really got a chance to go inside. She chose to wait outside the alley that led to the café. She had an urge to check her makeup – whatever remained of the kohl and pink lipstick she had briskly applied right before leaving home, but decided otherwise.

An otherwise quick dresser, Sam had changed over three outfits before deciding on the high neck, sleeveless, A-line top and a pair of blue faded, high-rise jeans. In the end she had decided to keep it simple, afraid she might look too over-the-top. She had not even worn the pair of heels that she had been thinking of wearing out all day long and chosen to go with her over worn sneakers. She was dressed for anything but a "date".

She recalled Rishabh's words. 'Be ready for the best date of your life,' he had told her.

'No, I cannot walk in with any expectations; it's just a friendly outing, completely platonic!' With that, she had wiped away the mascara too.

❖

'Mom, next time, please manage your grocery a little better,' Rishabh said snidely to his mom, handing over the bag full of vegetables, looking at his watch impatiently. He was running late.

'Oh, okay. Anything else I can do to make your life easier?' Mom had retorted, rolling her eyes. 'What are you running late for anyway? Is it a girl?' she said, her curiosity suddenly aroused. 'I do hope it's not *that* girl, Saloni, was it?'

'Oh god, mom! I'm going to pretend I didn't hear any of that. I'll see you later!' he yelled, frantically grabbing his house keys and making a run for the door.

He had missed the local as a result of this last-minute chore and the weekend crowd had ensured that he would have a hard time just getting in the next one. His first instinct was to carry a bunch of flowers for Sam, but he didn't want to give her the wrong impression.

What do you give someone you've never met before but the person has helped you out of serious crisis? He wondered.

He wasn't sure if carrying a souvenir along would be taken in a good stride by Sam and he did not want to risk souring her mood any further. He also hated the image that formed in his head with a bouquet in his hands.

'Sheesh! Not happening man!' On alighting off at Juhu, right before getting in an auto in an attempt to reach as fast as he could, Rishabh bumped into a young waif selling sunflowers. He instantly knew what he needed.

Rishabh got off outside the alley and quickly paid the auto driver. His eyes fell upon a girl dressed in white and blue, her beautiful black tresses were surrounded in a haze of smoke erupting from her lit cigarette. She was casually looking into her phone and taking another puff. Even in his wildest imagination, Rishabh had not anticipated finding her so attractive; so natural yet so stunning.

'Wow!' A sigh escaped his lips. Even from a distance, he knew this was Samira – the same features he had memorized the other night hunting down profile after profile on Facebook – he could recognize that face from any distance.

Suddenly self-conscious, Rishabh adjusted his collar and brushed his hair to make up for the damage the wind had caused. He briskly put his left hand behind his back and walked towards Sam, his steps faltering a little.

What's wrong with me? Please don't fall on your face! Just focus on walking, one foot after the other. He was in control of his gait and expressions and soon he was beside her.

The smoke reached his face before her eyes did. Sam had turned to her right as soon as she heard footsteps approaching her, blowing smoke right up Rishabh's nose. He sneezed, 'bless you,' she called out, slightly perturbed. He said a quick "thank you". She flicked away the remainder of her cigarette and scanned him involuntarily – black fitted shirt and blue denims with white sneakers. She instantly smiled, looking at their matching sneakers.

'Hello madam, are you just shy and looking down or am I not wearing any shoes?' He joked and looked down, his gleaming smile and dimples quickened the pace of her heart. The pink blotches he had noticed on her profile picture reappeared on her face.

'Nope, just relieved to see a somewhat regular guy. I actually wanted to meet to basically find out if I was being catfished by a nerdy teenager.' Rishabh laughed, throwing his head back a little.

'And? What is the verdict?' He asked, looking straight in her eyes, holding her gaze before blinking away.

'Well, at least the nerdy bit was true! she said, putting her hands in the back pocket of her jeans and tilting her head. She was challenging him to meet her eyes. He was pretty tall.

'So glad we recognized each other without having to decipher a code, or looking out for a dress code.' He laughed at his own joke and Sam smiled, finally feeling a little less nervous.

'I actually got you something. Sorry! You can totally throw it away, but I didn't want to come empty-handed,' he said, wrinkling his nose and raising his eyebrows quizzically. Sam couldn't help but look amused at his expression. She pursed her lips to control herself.

'Umm, okay, although sadly for you I come bearing no gifts.' She took her hands out of her pockets, exposing her bare hands. Rishabh slowly brought out the flower he had been hiding against his back. As if on cue, Samira's eyes lit up.

'Huh…a flower! Thanks, I guess?' She awkwardly took it in her hands, not knowing whether to smell it or stare at it.

'You can hold it closer, it's just a flower!' he said the words instead of actually laughing and instantly felt foolish.

'Yeah, I know! It's just that what about me told you that I may like sunflowers?' She said holding it a little closer, inspecting its petals.

'Well, you got me! But I really had no other bright ideas.' He rubbed the back of his neck.

'Thank you. Now, are we planning to stand here for the rest of the day? I thought you said there was a café nearby,'

❖

Inside the alley, Sam and Rishabh finally stumbled upon the open-garden café. Rishabh walked ahead as Sam slowed down, taking in the ambience of the place – the airy surroundings, the artisan, crafty lanterns, the huge tree growing right in the middle, the air charged with great music and conversations. Rishabh turned to see if she was still behind him when he found her smiling at the venue and him.

‘Do you like it?’ he asked, taking a step towards her.

‘It does have a nice vibe to it,’ she nodded in tune with the music. Rishabh could not help but grin.

‘But we’ll find out over food and drinks!’ She grinned back, the first since they met.

Seated at the table by the tree, the two ordered two servings of *keema pav*, Irish coffee, chocolate waffles with ice cream and a side of cheesy fries. Sam looked concerned at the amount of food Rishabh had ordered for them. He noticed her expression and laughed.

‘Don’t worry, it’s not a lot. I know it sounds like we ordered a lot for two people…’

‘You think?’ She raised her left eyebrow challenging him. He shook his head laughing.

‘Trust me. You won’t be able to resist,’ He winked and added, ‘I mean the food! Not me.’ He bit his lower lip still smirking.

‘Oh, thanks for clarifying. I will try my best to control myself,’ Sam replied, sarcasm dripping off her words. She gave in and laughed along with him.

‘So, what did happen with your robot finally? Is it still alive and well? Or did it run away with Sahil?’

‘Oh yes, that! First of all, thanks Sam. I honestly could not…’

'Yeah, yeah I know! Enough with that already. Tell me what happened,' she said and sat back in her chair. Rishabh chuckled and leaned towards her as he began telling her about his adventure of saving Bawarchi. He stopped talking after realizing that he had been talking non-stop for a couple minutes now. He grew nervous and began to say something, but decided otherwise.

Sam nodded and her gaze shifted from his face to her phone. Rishabh used the few seconds to study her face up close. She had minimal makeup and yet looked breathtakingly beautiful. She noticed him looking at her and blushed momentarily.

'What?' she asked, sitting up a little.

'Nothing,' he said with a shy smile. 'So how has your trip been so far? Oh wait, your grandmother was unwell, right? Is she better?'

'You remember!' She sounded genuinely surprised. 'My Nani is good. I honestly wonder if she was ever sick or if this was all a sham to get us to India! As for my trip, it's been all about sleeping and eating and hugging relatives who are virtually complete strangers. I haven't been out that much. In fact, this has been the first time ever that I have stepped out in Mumbai all by myself,' she boasted.

'Are you serious? I am so relieved that you reached here safely then! Did you find it difficult?' He asked, taking a sip of his water.

'Difficult? I literally walked a hundred odd steps. My Nani's place is just nearby. I never went out by myself because of obvious reasons – it's a grand family affair every time we visit, which is once in every four to five years. Everyone visits us – we're the VIPs really and are treated as such. Moreover, the jet lag leaves you worthless for a week. Even getting up is an achievement these days.' They were interrupted by the waiter who brought the dishes and drinks to their table. They take in the food, first with their eyes, then with their taste buds. Rishabh giggled to himself as they began eating.

'What? Your food's cracking jokes in your mouth?'

'Haha! No! I was just thinking about something funny – you are my first date who didn't click pictures of the food before eating it. I was just thinking how rare that is,'

Sam almost choked on the bite hearing the mention of the supposed "date" they were on again.

He really thinks we're on a date.

Rishabh asked, 'So how have your interviews been going well? Sorry, I wasn't around to ask or give you the pep talk all these weeks.'

Samira interrupted, 'Can you stop the "sorry-please and thank you" business. It's really getting almost too annoying now, you know. Look at us, finally here, catching up! Why do you have to keep bringing old squabbles up again and again?' She was intently leaning across from him, looking deep into his eyes.

Rishabh gave out an audible sigh before imitating her stance. 'I know. But it really scared me, Sam. Everything that happened. I didn't want to make it too awkward so I did not launch into a full-blown apology. But I do mean each "sorry" and "thank you".' He was relaxed after admitting this.

Sam touched his hands on the table on an impulse. A current ran through her body and she instantly folded her hands and brought them back under her chin. Rishabh had a similar strange look in his eyes.

Did he feel it too? Sam wondered.

For the next few minutes, they ate in silence, looking up at each other between bites, enjoying the food and communicating the same with animated expressions, taking in the ambience and the music. They were truly basking in the pleasant silence.

Sam finally broke the silence, asking Rishabh about his favourite hangouts, prodding him to divulge his preferred dishes and cuisine. She was surprised when he mentioned that he never had authentic Mediterranean food. She laughed over his awful puns, searching his dark eyes for things left unsaid when he suddenly broke off, mid-sentence, too frequently to her dismay.

Rishabh was giving in to her curiosity. He had only just noticed the husky and melodious tinge of her voice He failed to carry any thought till the end, getting distracted by the way she half-tucked her curls behind her ears as they came rolling back to her face.

He couldn't take his eyes off her.

18
Will they? Won't they?

'You realize you've been staring at me wordlessly for the last twenty seconds?' she asked him casually. He blushed.

'Sorry. I didn't know you were keeping track though.'

They were soon distracted by the waffles and ice cream that the waiter placed on their table and fought over every last morsel playfully. Later, they planned to move away for a smoke. Outside, Sam lit up her last cigarette. They shared swigs off it.

'So, I heard you broke up?' she asked, teasing, a mischievous smirk on her face.

'Oh yeah, wonder where you heard that?' he retorted, taking a step towards her. Sam stood resting her back against the wall of the café and Rishabh's face was just inches away from hers. She felt unnaturally shy and pushed him back with a hand on his chest. He held onto her hand for a few seconds. Then, he let it go. The air between them was charged with something other than plain chemistry. Crushing the cigarette with her shoe, Sam spoke.

'So, do you want to talk about it?' she asked, looking down at the cigarette butt.

'You really think I'll bring up the person who called you… that?' He had a bruised expression on his face and looked away. Sam noticed the change in his expression and decided to change the subject.

'I thought this was supposed to be the best date of my life.' Sam was feeling suddenly emboldened after that cigarette.

'So finally, you admit this is a date? Took you some time to figure it out, eh?' He leaned his upper body towards her, and looked into her eyes without blinking. 'The date's just begun, milady!' Rishabh winked at her.

Sam stood breathless and Rishabh had to tug at her hand to lead her back in.

He led her not to their table but to the quaint little bookshop that Sam had missed to notice.

'Wait what! There's a bookshop too?' Her eyes lit up and she walked excitedly towards it. Rishabh smiled and signaled to be back shortly as he headed to the café area to pay off their bill. A couple minutes later, Rishabh joined Sam inside the bookstore. Sam was already standing with a couple books in her hands.

'You're buying?' He asked, surprised.

'Yep!' She responded too engrossed in discovering titles and reading their blurbs.

'What is your favourite genre?' he asked, standing to a side, watching her with a bemused look on his face. Her focus was infectious and endearing.

'My favourite genre is whatever captivates my imagination.'

'Touché! Spoken like a true bibliophile!'

'What's yours?'

He brushed the back of his neck again. 'I'm a non-fiction guy myself.' He noticed the slight ridicule on her face and continued, 'I know, I'm not a fiction guy. Tried a hundred times, but reality reigns supreme.' He shrugged. He noticed how transparent Sam's face was – you could read every thought going through her mind on her face and yet, she posed an enigma to him. Happy with her purchases, Sam exited the shop with Rishabh in tow.

'This was the best moment of my day,' she said smiling at him.

'So far,' he replied. 'Although I should be a little hurt by that statement. I thought the best bit was meeting me and chomping on all that ravishing food!'

'You wish! The food comes to a close second,' she declared.

'So, what else do you have in mind?' She bit her lip, regretting the way her honest question sounded. 'I did not mean *that*,' she quickly overcame. Rishabh laughed and led her to the other side of the road, placing a hand on her back.

'Now we go for a walk along the sea, to digest the food that we gobbled up!'

He had hoped for her to throw tantrums or complain about the walking, the humidity or say something rude about the food, but Rishabh was pleasantly taken aback by her grace and approachability. He was smiling at her as she talked about Sahil.

'You should have stopped me, you know. I hate people who talk about their exes, but the topic just came about. Why am I even talking about him!' She shrugged with disgust.

'That's right!' They laughed.

At the beach, Rishabh chose cotton candy and Sam went for corn on the cob. A gust of wind blew Sam's hair into her eyes.

'Wow!' she exclaimed and Rishabh pushed it back with his free hand. Sam stepped back from him, suddenly frigid.

'What? I was just helping you, *baba*. Your hands were busy, with your books and the corn...'

'And this flower!' she completed his sentence. She suddenly grew quiet and focused on quickly finishing off the corn. 'Can we just sit quietly for some time?' she asked and began walking towards a clean spot by the sea without waiting for Rishabh's response.

'Are you tired?' he asked sitting beside her.

'No, Not at all.'

They watch the sunset sitting together, their feet buried in the cool sand. After a few minutes, Sam got up and walked towards the sea. Rishabh noticed her silhouette walking away from him and all he could suddenly think about was holding her tight in his arms.

No stupid moves, Rishabh. He warned himself. But a part of him could not help but stare at the beautiful woman who was walking along the shoreline. He let her be by herself for a while and got up when she waved him over.

Sam had been thinking about the hair brushing too. Why did he have to do that and why did I have to overreact? But I can't let this happen. It will be too difficult for both of us. She was fairly aware of the clear attraction between them. It was more than that; it was friendship and chemistry rolled up with care and respect. She knew Rishabh was special, but she couldn't lead him on. Finally beside her, Rishabh signed looking at the darkening sky.

'How long have we been out?' she asked, turning and looking at him.

'It's been almost three hours now.'

'Oh shoot! I have to be home for dinner.' They chuckled together at the mention of food. 'Yeah, it's going to be the longest and most challenging meal of my life.' She imagined herself sitting at another table, laden with food and felt like throwing up.

'Come, I'll walk you back.' Rishabh hesitated then added, 'if that is okay with you?'

Sam simply nodded and led the way.

❖

'So, when is your flight?' Rishabh was trying hard to make a regular conversation without upsetting her. He looked up through his long eyelashes and Sam's heart skipped a beat.

'Tomorrow night, actually early morning the day after,'

'So technically you are here another day.'

Hope – that is what she saw glimmering up in his eyes. She knew how dangerous that look was. Hence, she chose to stay quiet. They silently walked towards her place. She fumbled with words for a bit as Rishabh looked on, hoping for her to break the silence, but he stayed disappointed.

I need to tell her. How else would she know? Maybe this is right, maybe this can happen.

He looked at her and almost saw the thoughts rushing through her head. She seemed to be struggling with something heavy and he wished for a way to unburden her. Their hands slightly brushed and the heat radiated on their faces. Rishabh put his hands in his jeans pockets and Sam clutched the wilted sunflower in both her hands. The air between them was heavy. They desperately wanted to say to each other, but couldn't bring themselves to admit.

The house was only a short walk and they were now only a couple meters away.

'This was good! Thanks, I had a good time.' Sam suddenly slowed down to a complete halt. They were still out of anyone's view from the house. She fidgeted with her hair a little and steadied herself.

To Rishabh's surprise, Sam had a strangely confident look on her face. Her eyes did not radiate the smile that was plastered on her face. Was she really saying goodbye? He wanted to clutch her tight, feel her skin on his, smell the infusion of their breaths and breathe in the scent of her hair.

Sam could feel the current in the air between them. He was standing just inches away from her. She wanted to hug him tight, but that would bring down her façade. Just a quick goodbye would be best. She saw Rishabh searching her face for something she had tucked away in a corner inside her.

This is the best thing, for both of us. Just take a deep breath and walk away, Sam. But that look!

Rishabh extended a hand towards her that Sam blocked.

'No, Rishabh, please don't,' It took every ounce of her self-control, but she let go of his hand. 'We shouldn't. It's better we don't do something we both regret,'

'But...' Rishabh moved closer towards her in an attempt to hold her face in his hands.

'I don't know when I'll see you again, Rishabh,' Sam interjected, her eyes holding an entire ocean of regret. She took a step back.

'But Sam...'

'No, it's not right. For either of us. I'm sorry I can't do this. Bye.' Sam turned away and started to run towards her house.

'Sam, don't do this. We can work it out. Please come back! I...' Rishabh called out and paused as he saw her slow down and finally stop. He jogged up to her but stopped a few steps away. Sam was still turned away from him, taking in his voice.

Imbued with a new spirit, Rishabh confidently declared, 'We both know we like each other, Sam. I know you feel it too! It's so obvious – we are perfect. Please, let's...'

Before he could finish his sentence, Sam ran back the distance between them and embraced him. He held her face up as her hands traveled up his back, neck and hair.

'Let's make it work,' he said before bending his head and grazing her lips with his. The softness of their touch made Sam tremble all over and give up the last straws of her constraint. Her lips hungrily found his again.

Stopping for a breath, she said, 'If you want me to stop, tell me now.' There was a tenacious look in her eyes that he had never seen before.

'I'll be mad to stop the most salacious kiss of my life!' That made Sam relax and giggle against his mouth. His breath was hot. She kissed him again, his tongue teasingly prodding hers. He wrapped his hands around her waist, her hands traced his spine.

'How?' she asked, coming up for breath again.

'What?' He asked quite out of breath himself. That kiss had surely made him forget everything. He quickly kissed her nose, smiling wide.

'Before, you said let's make it work. How?' She looked deep in his dark eyes, afraid she had burst their bubble.

'Well, there's something I forgot to mention before,' he rubbed the back of his neck. 'I received an invite to Stanford's Incubator Program for next year.' Sam's eyes widened in disbelief. 'And, I've decided to accept it.' He said, leaving a quick peck on her parted lips.

'You jerk!' Sam slapped his arm. 'I'll kill you.' She glared at him, the lower half of her face giving away her delight.

'That you certainly can and will,' he said and smiled and they kissed again, passion unbridled.

'So, wait for me, don't forget me, okay? Just a year,' he said tenderly against her bruised lips, pulling her lower lip with his teeth.

'Then this kiss better last a year!' she said.

Epilogue

'I need more supplies!' Saloni yelled.

'There you go, babe,' CaptainJack said running towards the only girl on the game screen.

'I've got some extra ammo, just in case,' BraveWolf ran up just a second later.

'I have enough for now. Hey, DragonWings, how do you like my look?' Saloni asked seductively.

All the avatars stopped and waved at her.

DragonWings sent a peach emoji her way. She led their way, firing a submachine gun.

Three months after her breakup with Rishabh, Saloni had not only mastered BOA, but also the art of flirting on online gaming apps.

Shooting at the last of their enemies, she yelled, 'I am Spartacus!'